D1242074

A MASS FOR THE DEAD

3 1705 00364 3548

A MASS FOR THE DEAD

SUSAN MCDUFFIE

FIVE STAR

An imprint of Thomson Gale, a part of The Thomson Corporation

Serving Every Ohioan
Library Center

State
Library
of Ohio
Knowledge. Power. Opportunity.

SEO Library Center
40780 Marietta Road
Caldwell, OH 43724

THOMSON

GALE™

Detroit • New York • San Francisco • New Haven, Conn. • Waterville, Maine • London

Copyright © 2006 by Susan McDuffie.

ALL RIGHTS RESERVED
This novel is a work of fiction. Names, characters, places and incidents are either the product of the author's imagination, or, if real, used fictitiously.
No part of this book may be reproduced or transmitted in any form or by any electronic or mechanical means, including photocopying, recording or by any information storage and retrieval system, without the express written permission of the publisher, except where permitted by law.
Set in 11 pt. Plantin.

LIBRARY OF CONGRESS CATALOGING-IN-PUBLICATION DATA

McDuffie, Susan.
  A mass for the dead / Susan McDuffie. — 1st ed.
    p. cm.
  ISBN 1-59414-489-3 (alk. paper)
    1. Monks—Crimes against—Fiction. 2. Scotland—History—14th century—
Fiction. I. Title.
  PS3613.C396M37 2006
  813'.6—dc22   2006020127

U.S. Hardcover:
ISBN 13: 978-1-59414-489-9
ISBN 10: 1-59414-489-3

First Edition. First Printing: November 2006.

Published in 2006 in conjunction with Tekno Books and Ed Gorman.

Printed in the United States of America on permanent paper
10 9 8 7 6 5 4 3 2 1

ACKNOWLEDGMENTS

First, I must thank my parents, Bruce and Winifred McDuffie. Their loving parenting over the years has immeasurably enriched my life and nurtured my creativity. Bob and June Stevens encouraged me, read the manuscript and kept me at it. Donna Thomson also read the manuscript and made many helpful suggestions, as did members of the Santa Fe Writers Group. Sheila F. Duffy's booklet, *Colonsay and Oronsay,* provided initial seeds, which eventually grew to fruition in this story. Any errors are entirely my own.

CAST OF CHARACTERS

On Colonsay

Muirteach (Moor-tech) MacPhee
Somerled, his dog
Seamus, Muirteach's fourteen-year-old friend
Aorig, Seamus's mother
Seamus's father
Gillespic, Muirteach's uncle, Chief of the Clan MacPhee
Euluasaid, his wife
Sheena, the Prior's mistress
Angus and Alasdair, her brothers
Sean, Maire and baby Columbanus, Sheena's children
Donald Dubh (doo), tavern keeper
His wife
Tormod, a mason
His mother

On Oronsay and at the Priory

Crispinus, the Prior of Oronsay and Muirteach's father
Gillecristus, the sub-prior
Columbanus, the baker, Sheena's brother
Donal, the librarian
Padraig, the beekeeper
Moloug, the brewer
Augustus

Aidan
Gillecolm
Alasdair Beag, an islander
Calum Glas, master mason
Eogain, Tormod's brother

On Islay

John MacDonald, the Lord of the Isles
Fearchar (farcher) Beaton, a physician
Mariota, his daughter
Robbie, Mariota's cousin
Seòras, a harper
Muirteach's great-aunt Morag
Cousin Eilidh (aylee)
Alsoon
Padraic, a priest on Nave Island
Iain Mor and Niall Sgadan, two brothers, fishermen, on Nave
  Island

On Mull

Lachlan Lubanach MacLean
Lady Mary, his wife

GLOSSARY

Amadan (fm. *Amadain*): fool

Bairn: a child

Birlinn: Scottish galley, varying in size from a few to many oars.

Brat: mantle

Cailleach: old hag, also the name of the whirlpool now known as the Corryvreckan

Dia: God

Each Uisge: water horse

Eilean: island

Gille Mor: sword bearer

Iorram: a rowing song

Léine: saffron shirt, made of linen

Luchd-tighe: chief's bodyguard

Mazer: drinking cup

Merk: a unit for measuring land

Mether: wooden square-sided drinking cup

Mo chridhe: (mo cree) my heart

Nabhaig: a small boat

Nathrach: serpent

Quaich: round saucer-like drinking cup

Sgian dubh: dagger

Sithichean: the faerie

Glossary

Uisgebeatha: whiskey (literally, the water of life)
Ùruisg: goblin

AUTHOR'S NOTE

Gillespic, Crispinus, and John MacDonald, the Lord of the Isles, actually existed. Their personalities and Crispinus's various wives, children, and other activities are totally invented, as is Muirteach. The MacPhee clan was the hereditary "Keepers of the Records" for the Lords of the Isles, and, in part, this book came from my desire to tell the story of how this might have come about.

The rhymes and charms in this book were taken from the *Carmina Gadelica,* collected by Alexander Carmichael in the 1800s, except for the verse in the last chapter, which was invented. Readers wishing to know more about the Lordship of the Isles might enjoy reading *The Lords of the Isles* by Ronald Williams, which gives a good overview of this period in Scottish history.

MAP OF
COLONSAY AND ORONSAY

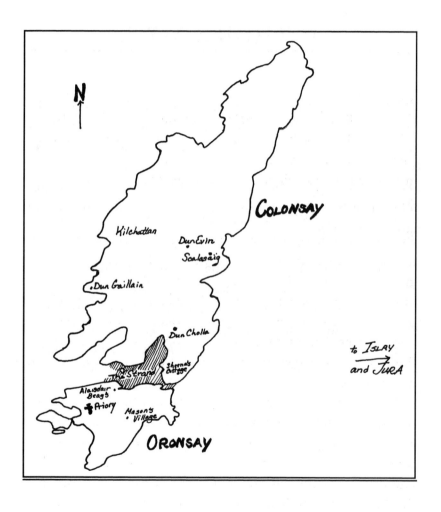

PROLOGUE

Scotland 1373

The body floated, limbs tangled in strands of reddish dulse and yellow bladderwrack. Salt water washed over it, then receded. The tide left the flotsam lying on wet sand, sightless eyes staring into obscurity and fingers just grazing the large stone Celtic cross that stood halfway across the Strand.

A hungry gull alighted, and pecked at one eye with interest. Others joined it, eager for breakfast, and their cries rang through the salt-smelling air as they fought over the carrion. The first gull, satiated, took flight as the sky lightened and the sun began to rise. Beating its wings against the damp air, the bird circled over the expanse of wet sand, pooled water and black rocks that now separated the tidal island of Oronsay and its gray stone Priory from the larger green hills and more mundane concerns of Colonsay.

The sun tried to burn through the mist, but failed, leaving the body wrapped wetly in fog like a winding sheet, with the keening of the gulls for a requiem. It wasn't until Alasdair Beag came down to dig oysters for the monks and nearly bumped into the corpse, that his brethren learned what had happened to the Prior and why it was that he had not shown his face at Matins the night before.

Chapter 1

A sprig of heather poked me in the side. Unable to ignore it, I tossed and burrowed into the piled heather and bracken covered with a blanket that served as my bed, trying in vain to find a more comfortable spot. So Seamus found me awake that morning, when he came to tell me my father was dead.

I sat up and stared at him. Seamus's fourteen-year-old form looked dark against the morning light from the open door of the blackhouse behind him.

"Muirteach, did you no hear me?" He shook me again. "I said your father's dead."

My dog woke from the noise, rose, and licked my face, by way of a morning greeting.

"No, now, Seamus," I said. I patted Somerled's large shaggy head a bit absently before I waved the dog away, thinking Seamus must somehow have gotten the news wrong. "That's never true."

"No, it is true, Muirteach. You must be believing me."

"No," I said again, stupidly, but something in Seamus's high-pitched tone, his voice just cracking as he spoke, stopped me in mid-phrase, and made me begin to believe the lad.

"What was it?" I asked, after another moment, my mind racing. "A fit?"

"No." Seamus paused. "He was murdered."

My hands went cold, and I almost choked on my own spit. "Murdered?"

"Aye."

I wondered which of his women had finally killed him. The Prior of Oronsay, dead.

I stood up, and began to dress, pulling my linen shirt over my head and throwing my *brat* over my shoulders. The rough wool of it fell about me warmly in the morning chill.

I watched Seamus squat on my stool next to the remains of the fire on the open hearth. The morning sun filtered through the doorway of the blackhouse and picked out a few details, my leather satchel thrown carelessly on the floor, Seamus's brown hair untidy, the sharp angles and freckles of his boy's face.

I thought of my own father's face, his voice, scornful when he spoke of his bastard son. I would never hear that voice again.

"What else do you know of it, Seamus?" I finally asked him when I could speak.

"A messenger came from the Priory, for your uncle, and himself told me to fetch you. He has already gone to the canons, on his galley." Seamus's words tumbled out, one upon the other, in his eagerness to tell me the tale. Stunned, I stood and listened, trying to make sense of what he said.

"Old Alasdair found him. He'd gone down to get oysters, but there he was—the Prior, I mean," added Seamus unnecessarily. "Facedown in the Strand he was, with his hands nearly touching the Sanctuary Cross."

I filled the basin with water from the jug that sat by the hearth, splashed some on my face, and took a drink.

"His mouth was full of sand. He'd been choked with it," Seamus added.

I gagged and spat the water out upon the hearth. It sizzled on some still-warm embers and I watched a faint trail of white steam rise, watched it wend its way up and out through the darkness of the thatch overhead, while I fought down my desire to be sick.

Seamus picked up a stick, tracing idle designs in the ashes. "You'll be wanting a fire," he finally said, awkwardly, to break the silence. He poked at the peat in the fire pit. "It's cold this morning."

"I'll be wanting to see him, I'm thinking, not a fire." I spoke more harshly than I'd realized and Seamus put the stick down hastily. "Where is he?"

"They took the body to the Priory."

Aye, I thought, with some bitterness. Where else would they take him? Certainly not here, to his own son.

"We'd best be going then, Seamus. That is, if you're coming with me."

The lad nodded eagerly. I found his hero-worship oddly comforting this morning, misplaced though it seemed most of the time.

I grabbed another drink of water from the wooden cup that sat by the jug, and managed to swallow it this time.

"Let's be off then," I said and lifted aside the flap of cowhide that served as a door on my fine house.

"I will just be telling my mother," Seamus said, darting next door. I nodded. Somerled tried to follow, but I told him to stay and for once he obeyed me, whining a bit as he skulked back inside the hut.

The brightness of the June day was blinding after the dimness inside my hut and I stood for a moment outside, waiting for Seamus and letting my eyes adjust.

The village of Scalasaig looked much as usual this morning, the stone huts, with their heather thatch, snug against the damp and the breezes from the bay. I smelled the scent of peat fires and baking, mingled with the more aromatic smells of my neighbors' middens.

With two bannocks in his hands, Seamus emerged from the house he shared with his mother and father. He crammed a bannock into his mouth while we set out walking.

"Mother gave me this for you," he said between mouthfuls, handing me the other bannock. "She said you should be eating something."

Earlier that morning, in the street leading through the center of the village, cattle going to pasture and folk going about their business had already churned up the mud to a fine morass. We left and headed south, down the track leading through the low hills the two miles or so to the Strand.

The dew hung heavy on the bracken and pink thistle that lined the track. Among green rushes and bog cotton, a single yellow iris stood alone and I marveled at the beauty of it. Perhaps it was the shock of that morning that made me notice it so, petals curling away from the center of the flower, dew drops dripping from the softness of them like crystal tears.

Mist rolled in as we passed Loch Colla, muffling sound and sight so that we could not even see the walls of the Church of the Glen. The lowing of some cattle grazing in the uplands echoed mournfully. I shivered, my bad leg began to ache, and I wished I had thought to borrow a horse. We saw few people about. Even the death of the Prior of Oronsay, and himself an island man, wasn't enough to drag most folk from their tasks on this June day.

"It was your uncle, Muirteach, that told me of it. He said to come and find you."

I realized Seamus was speaking. I had not been listening.

"And himself?" I asked, finally, trying to collect my thoughts. "Where is the MacPhee?"

"He'll aye be there now, settling it all with the brothers."

That was right, I remembered. Seamus had already told me my uncle had gone on his galley to see to things at the Priory.

And good luck to him there. My uncle Gillespic was always one to try and get things settled, one way or another, as quickly as ever might be. But the death of his own brother, a prior, for all that he had had two handfasted wives, a full-grown bastard son, and some other bastards as well, might not be so easily settled.

"The MacDonald will be needing to know of it all," I commented darkly, "and he'll not be pleased."

The sun glowed brighter, burning through the remnants of the fog, against the hill behind us to the east. To the west, I saw the green bulk of Oronsay across the Strand and beyond that the sea towards Ireland.

We made our way past the glistening black rocks that lined the Strand. Seamus headed for the old coracle beached on the damp sand. "The brothers will not mind if we take this over."

"No," I agreed. "They'll be thinking of other things the now."

We pushed the boat into the water and jumped in. The tide was full in and just starting to turn. I glimpsed the stone bulk of the carved Sanctuary Cross standing above the waters, marking the boundary between secular and sacred land. I thought of my father lying there dead, and shuddered.

The heavy wooden weight of the oars in my hand comforted me. Strange I should feel it so, the death of a father who had only tolerated me at best. At worst, I had always felt he hated me. I had not been the son he'd hoped for, and he had made no secret of it. A cripple, good for nothing except scriving, and hating that. And being a cripple, I had not even had the grace to settle quietly into the life of the Priory, as would have been only proper and seemly. Neither a fish nor a fowl. The spray touched my cheek like a benediction but I pulled hard at the oars, trying to outrow my thoughts.

The bottom of the coracle scraped the sandy bottom as we neared the other side. I pulled it onto the bank and followed Seamus up the hill towards the Priory, feeling the rays of the sun hit the back of my legs with a faint warmth as I walked, the water and sand drying off in the cold wind.

The sun struck the gray stone walls as we crested the hill and passed piles of stone lying on the grass, ready for the masons. No workers were about and I guessed they would not labor today. Behind the walls, we could see the newly finished chapel, chapter house, and cloisters, all built of the same stone. Inside the new chapel, with its fine slate roof, candles burned, their light glowing through the tall slit windows, but we turned towards the infirmary.

"That's where he'll be, I'm thinking," said Seamus, his fourteen-year-old bravado somewhat cowed by the atmosphere of the Priory. Having lived here for ten years I did not share his illusions, and led the way past the dormitory to the infirmary. I did not see my uncle, or the sub-prior. Perhaps they spoke privately on the event.

My steps slowed, not wanting to see what I knew awaited me, yet fascinated, too; that awful fascination one feels for the final mystery.

And may he rot in whatever Hell he's gone to, I found myself thinking as I finally gazed on the sandy, dirtied body of my father. It lay on a plinth, the rough boards covered with a linen cloth, while next to it a canon chanted prayers for the dead. The body lay on its back, pale, waxen, looking in some weird stony fashion like a grave-slab carving. It was my father, and yet not my father.

The gulls had gotten to the body, before Alasdair Beag had found him, and the corpse was the worse for it. A bloody depressed area on his head showed where someone had struck him, from behind. His face and neck had an ugly, bluish cast to them, and a fine thin mark around his neck looked pale by comparison with the surrounding skin. His neck and jaw were bruised, his mouth stuffed with sand. Grains of sand spilled out from his mouth onto his lips.

Whoever had done this had battered him after stuffing the sand in, hitting again and again. Some seaweed still lay tangled in his hands and the hair around his tonsure lay wetly against the cold skin. My own throat closed and I felt myself choking as I looked at the body.

I covered the body again with the linen sheet and turned to go. Tears filled my eyes. I swallowed them tightly. He was dead, and I need never bear the humiliation of hearing him refer to me as "his bastard son, the cripple" again.

My uncle stopped me as I left the infirmary.

"Muirteach."

"Aye, Uncle?"

During the years I had spent in his home as his foster son I had learned to be wary of Uncle Gillespic when he had that tone in his voice, and I was not wrong now. He pulled me to one side, just inside the dormitory, empty except for old Brother Augustus, where we could speak more privately.

"Wait outside for us Seamus, there's a good lad," Gillespic dismissed the lad and turned towards me, his hand on my arm for comfort.

My uncle was a broad-shouldered man, with long chestnut hair and a full beard, and penetrating eyes that now rested upon me thoughtfully a moment before he spoke again.

"This is a bad thing, Muirteach, very bad, I'm thinking."

I shrugged my shoulders, not wanting to show him my feelings, but my uncle continued. "The MacDonald will not be liking it."

"And so? It does not matter if he likes it or no, the man is dead, Uncle." I must have sounded more sullen than I meant to, for Gillespic stopped for a moment and looked me full in the face.

"And harder on you than you'd admit."

I nodded, forced to the admission by his gaze. Sure, that was one of the talents of my uncle, that gift of seeing the best in you that you'd been trying to hide, even from yourself. As a boy fostered into his household, those years before I had gone to the Priory, my uncle's hazel eyes had seemed to see right to the root of my soul, somehow finding good in his crippled and angry nephew.

It was a pity my father hadn't shared that trait. The hot lump in my throat got the better of me for a minute, and I looked away and out the dormitory door, studying the new carvings on the pillars of the cloister, until my eyes cleared.

"Well, it's as I said, Muirteach," my uncle continued in a kinder tone. "The MacDonald himself will not be liking this, his own Prior killed in his own backyard, so to say, and will be wanting some answers to it. And for myself, he was my brother after all, and I'll be having to ask the honor-price from whoever is responsible. Or you should be asking."

"I'm asking for nothing," I said stubbornly.

"Who did do it, then?" I asked, after a moment when my uncle did not answer. "Do they know?"

Gillespic shook his head. "Nary a clue. Just a big bloody blow to his skull, and a mouth choked full with sand, like, with not a person nearby to see or hear anything at all, at all."

"That's always the way of it," I said with much more nonchalance than I felt. I shuddered, unable to keep up the pretence. "My mother's kin, they could have done it."

"Aye, or Sheena's kin, or even yourself. Crispinus had a rare talent for making enemies." My uncle crossed himself and added, "God rest his soul," in a rare show of piety, yet somehow I sensed it was heartfelt. Then he stared at me suddenly with those remarkable eyes he had. "Where were you, the last night?"

"At home, drinking."

"Alone then."

"Seamus was with me. And Aorig saw me." I was suddenly

angry. "What are you saying, Uncle? By Christ's Holy Blood, I had no reason to love my father, but I did not kill him, if that's what you're thinking."

Brother Augustus looked up at us sharply as he heard my outburst, but my uncle continued without sparing the monk a glance.

"No, now, Muirteach," Gillespic said soothingly, "I'm not saying that at all. Muirteach, you must control yourself the now, and not be swearing here in the Priory. You'll be giving the poor brothers here fits, as if it were not bad enough for them to have a dead prior to be dealing with."

Brother Augustus returned to his prayers and after another minute my uncle continued. "Every man knows you had little reason to love your father, what with the way he treated your poor mother, God rest her soul. And you, as well. And for that, I'm thinking you might come under suspicion, that's all of it."

"Well, Uncle, you can rest your mind. I did not do it. And whyever should I, with half of the population of the Isles ready to do it for me?"

Gillespic shook his head. "It's a bad thing, that it is Muirteach. And I'm thinking you should be the one to carry the news to His Lordship himself."

"Me?"

"Aye, whoever better to do it than the man's oldest son."

And whoever better to do it than someone not my uncle, I thought, but I kept my thoughts to myself. Gillespic had that amazing quality, he could get you to do something you had no desire to do, and somehow you'd find yourself happy to be doing it for him. And, even though I protested, I knew I'd be setting sail before much more time had passed, southward towards Islay, to take the news to the Lord of the Isles.

CHAPTER 2

Gillespic had a small *birlinn* readied, twelve oars only, and we set off from Oronsay, after a hurried meal. Or rather, I set off, accompanied by four other men to crew the galley. Seamus was eager to come along, and a good hand with the oars. Gillespic stayed behind.

Clouds obscured the early sun of the day, and soon it started raining, a misty drizzle that strengthened, soaked through my shirt and cloak, and made me shiver. The *iorram* sung by the crew was a sad one, suited to the day, and the dreary errand we were on made my mood worse.

When I tried to imagine him gone, I found that I could not fathom life without my father. He had loomed large in my life. As a child I tried to win his approval, but had never found it coming.

My thoughts were bitter and I took a swig from the flask I carried by way of escaping them, then munched on a bannock when I wasn't rowing, tasting the salt from the sea spray in my mouth along with the oatcake.

Despite the rain we made good enough time and by the time we reached the Sound of Islay the rain let up a bit. You could just make out the Paps of Jura, gray-humped through the mist on our left, but looking behind us the green bulk of Colonsay had vanished in the clouds.

It was getting on towards the evening when we beached the *birlinn* at Coal Ila, wet, cold, and hungry. The few small stone huts, their thatch dripping wetly after the rain, looked quiet. We could find no one there to rent us horses and so we set off on foot towards Finlaggan, where we would find John MacDonald, Lord of the Isles.

We made good enough time, and I kept up well enough with the others, at a walk. The hills of Islay gleamed green after the rain and the air smelled fresh and cold. I had been born here, but remembered little of it for all that. After my mother had died, and I'd been sent to Uncle Gillespic's for fostering, I hadn't returned often and this side of the island was far from the Rhinns, where my mother and I had lived with her family. But Finlaggan I knew well enough, having often accompanied Gillespic here in these last years since I'd left the Priory, and it was with a sense of dread that I saw the loch and the islands grow nearer as we walked.

The track grew busy as we neared the settlement, and the smell of peat fires rose from the cluster of houses by the loch side. We saw miners, along with others, craftsmen and lead workers, returning to their homes and their evening meals after the day's work.

I was feeling an uncomfortable knot in my stomach. I cursed Gillespic for sending me on this errand, and cursed myself for accepting it. Not that I would have refused Gillespic, I admitted to myself wryly after I had finished cursing. I worshipped my foster father. But now I had to tell the MacDonald about the death of my own father.

The stone and wattle houses of the village spilled over on both sides of the causeway and down along the sides of the loch. Many of the homes belonged to His Lordship's own elite bodyguard, the *luchd-tighe*, while others housed craftsmen serving the castle, and miners from the silver and lead mines. On the loch itself, nestled like jewels in a blue setting, we saw the two islands that formed the Lord's castle of Finlaggan—Eilean

Mor, the big island, and beyond that the smaller Council Island, Eilean nan Comhairle.

The Lord of the Isles, a descendant of that same Somerled my dog was named for, ruled a vast confederacy of clans in the Highlands and Hebrides, foremost among them his own Clan Donald. In his own territories John MacDonald had nearly as much power as the Stewart monarch himself, for the King in Edinburgh was a distant figure who had little to do with our life in the islands. However, with that same canniness that he had shown when he put aside his first wife, Amie MacRuari, to marry the Stewart's own daughter, John MacDonald signed his documents and decrees merely *Dominus Insularium,* the Lord of the Isles, and had sworn at least nominal fealty to the Stewart king.

The pit of my stomach felt worse with thinking about it all, and my leg started to ache again as we neared the causeway. The sentry by the entrance was my distant cousin, Fergus, and he let us pass by without protest. We passed the kitchen buildings, where the aroma of roasting venison mingled with the smell of peat smoke to make me aware of how hungry I was after the long day, and then the jetty and the stone bulk of the Great Hall reared before us. The MacDonald's men waited by the door, idly fingering their broadswords when they saw us.

"We're needing to see the MacDonald," I said. "It's the MacPhee sent us, with news from Colonsay."

The sentry raised an eyebrow. "News, is it then?" I nodded, but didn't enlighten him as to what it was. "He's away. Hunting," he added, after a minute.

"Come away in, then," he continued, looking a bit disappointed, when we still did not enlighten him. "Perhaps himself will be seeing you when he returns. Or perhaps he will be wanting to wait until after the meal."

We were settled and brought some food and drink. After

26

waiting for over an hour in the smoky, crowded hall, drinking claret, watching some MacNeills playing at draughts, His Lordship's grizzled hound scratch at his fleas, and half-listening while a harper played idly in a corner of the hall, I concluded that himself would be seeing us after the meal. Or I hoped so. The rumbling in my stomach had grown more insistent, despite the bannocks and cheese we had been given, and I hoped the meal would come first and that the telling of our news, and my encounter with His Lordship, could wait.

There was a stir in the hall and the MacDonald entered, followed by his tail of retainers, his *gille mor,* or sword bearer, members of his *luchd-tighe,* and a number of other clansmen and followers, all talking roisterously of the hunt they had had and calling for ale.

Two of them struggled to carry in a dead stag, which they heaved to the floor of the hall. The old hound got up and sniffed interestedly at it, but the men shooed him away, and he limped over to rejoin the other hounds, now settling in a corner of the space.

The MacDonald was not a tall man, dark haired and dark eyed, showing more of the Celt than the Norse in his looks. He was dressed for the hunt, but the wool of his *brat* was of a fine weave, fastened with a large jewel-encrusted pin of gold, and he wore boots of the finest leather. His keen eyes sought us out in the hall. Apparently the sentry had told him of our arrival. After a moment he signaled for me to join him where he sat on a finely carved wooden chair before the peat fire, drinking ale from a *mether* made of silver and ivory.

"Your Lordship," I began, not knowing if he would remember me, but he did.

"Muirteach, is it? What is this news from Colonsay?"

"It's Prior Crispinus. My father." I stopped speaking a moment to swallow, my throat gone suddenly dry.

"Well, what of him?"

"He's dead. He was murdered." I heard the silence behind me, followed quickly by the beginnings of shocked converse in the hall.

"Saint's blood," he swore, almost starting up out of his chair. His eyes narrowed, and he settled in his seat again. "Who did it?"

I shrugged my shoulders in answer to his question.

"Rome will not be happy. Nor the King, I'm thinking." He thought, taking a sip from his glass. "Especially if no one is held accountable."

He looked at me, his gray eyes keen. "Tell me what happened," he commanded.

I told him, at least what we knew of it all.

"His fingers just touching the Sanctuary Cross." His Lordship drained his ale. He wiped his mouth with a fine napkin of richly embroidered linen. "It's an abomination, that is. Sacrilege."

He looked at me again, and I felt like a bull at a summer cattle fair. "Muirteach, you are his son. And you've a good mind in you, and are not ill-favored, for all that you—" He hesitated, his eyes going to my leg for a moment.

"For all that I cannot run," I finished for him.

"Aye, well, there is that. But, as I've said, you've a good mind, and you can read, and write. Aye, you'll be just the man I'm needing."

Now my eyes narrowed. For when the MacDonald said he needed you, you got suspicious, for all that he was called *Buachaill nan Eilean,* the Herdsman of the Isles.

"Yes?" was all I said.

His Lordship called to his henchman for claret, but did not answer me immediately. The man brought the wine, and set it on a small table within easy reach of His Lordship's chair.

The Lord of the Isles poured wine into two silver goblets and offered me one.

"Aye, you'll be the man for it, being his son and all as well." He looked at me, measuring me. "I want you to find the killer. And once justice is done, then we can write to Rome. And the King. There's no need to be troubling them before we know who killed him."

"They'll hear, at least the King will, in Edinburgh, with his daughter your wife." There was no point in arguing about the other. I would have to find my father's killer. The MacDonald was right, it was my duty as a son, for all that I had not loved my father. And now it was my duty to my clan's overlord as well; he had just made it so.

His Lordship smiled. "Aye. Best you write the King, then, and bring it to me when you are done. Away in the back room with you now. I'll see to it that you've parchment and pen. And a light. You can be writing to the King before the meal, and then—"

"What am I to write?"

"Simple."

I groaned. It did not sound simple to me, but the MacDonald continued. "Tell him the Prior has been killed, and that we are close to finding the murderer. And when we have brought him to justice we will be letting him know of it. Oh, and send greetings from my wife." He beamed. "I'll send Fergus with the letter. He's been wanting to see Edinburgh. Or is the King at Rothesay the now?"

He left. My stomach growled. A servant ushered me into the back room of the hall, where I found a table, illuminated by the fading evening light shining through the slit window, and the same henchman soon brought writing materials and a candle, just as the MacDonald had promised.

"And bring some more claret," I told him, as I sharpened the quill and attempted to compose the letter. The end result, I told myself, was none so bad, for all that I had never written to a King before.

To His Majesty King Robert II the Steward of Scotland
From John MacDonald, Dominus Insularium,
Lord of the Isles
Greetings: We desire you to know as soon as ever we could inform our Royal Father of the sad events which have here transpired at Oronsay Priory on this day June the 27, 1373. Our beloved Prior of Oronsay, Crispinus MacPhee, has been found done to death in a cruel manner by some criminal as yet unknown. As we do not wish to cause any undue concern to our well-loved royal father, we hasten to assure him of our intent to bring the perpetrator of such an infamous deed to justice, and that right soon, and communicate with you at such time as that has been done. In addition I hasten to assure you that my lady-wife, your own daughter Margaret, rests well and sends you all kind greetings.

Now it only remained to catch the murderer, I thought wryly. The servant reappeared and, finding I had finished, left again to summon the MacDonald. He inspected the letter and was well pleased, clapping me on the back, and walking with me to the main room where the tables had been set up and the meal already underway.

Seated at the far end of a lower table, I ate my fill at last. Venison, salmon, oatcakes, bannocks, cheese, honey and curds. Mead and claret. I had just about reached my limit when I saw the MacDonald gesture to a tall, thin, older man and motion in my direction. By this time the pages were removing the dishes, and people had begun to mill about. So I was not too surprised when the man approached me a short while later. He had a slight stoop, from time spent over books perhaps, and blond hair going a bit to gray, but his blue eyes when he looked at me were clear and penetrating, his manner calm and soothing.

"You are Muirteach MacPhee?" he inquired.

"Aye. I am."

"Himself was wanting myself to accompany you back to Colonsay. I am Fearchar Beaton, the physician."

We knew of Fearchar Beaton, in Colonsay. He was famous all over the Isles, as all the Beatons were, for their knowledge.

The story goes that one of them, while walking down the road carrying a fine hazel staff, had been approached by a strange gentleman. The man asked where the Beaton had gotten his hazel staff, then asked the Beaton to return to that same hazel tree, and watch a hole beneath it, where he would see six serpents leave, and then return, the white adder coming last. The Beaton was to catch this last serpent and bring it to the gentleman.

The Beaton agreed, and found all as the strange gentleman had promised at the hazel tree. When he returned to the gentleman, with the white adder carefully stopped up in a bottle, the man was delighted. Opening the bottle, he flung the serpent into a pot he had boiling by the roadside. He then asked the Beaton to watch the pot for a wee while, as he had to leave, and on no account to let it boil over.

The Beaton did so, but the pot boiled furiously, and he could not stop it. He reached for the lid, burned his finger with some of the potion, and put his finger in his mouth. The eyes of his wisdom were opened, and he understood the language of beasts, and plants, which were helpful to the sick and infirm, and the healing of every ache and pain that man is known to suffer.

I am not knowing if that story is true, but sure enough it is that all the Beatons are renowned healers and physicians. None are better. Some have even studied in far off Spain, and in

Paris. But whyever would the MacDonald be wanting the Beaton to return to Colonsay with me?

The Beaton himself answered my question, before I could ask it.

"Himself is wanting me to look at the body, to see what I can tell about the manner of his death," he said. "The body of the Prior. Is it your father, lad?"

I bristled a bit, whether it was from being called lad, or from the kind tone of voice the man had, I did not know.

"Aye. I am his bastard."

"No shame in that. It is the man who makes his own way in the world, not his father."

I shrugged my shoulders. Perhaps. "When do you want to be going?"

"First light tomorrow. I'm not wanting to wait too long to see it. We could almost go tonight." For this close to midsummer the sky still held some light, even so close to midnight as it was.

"The crew is tired. As I am."

He did not rankle at my tone. "Well, then, you will sleep, and we will leave in the morning. Tell your crew. Was no one telling you where you can bide?"

"In the hall here, I'm guessing. Or in the guest house." The feast showed no signs of stopping at any point soon.

The Beaton nodded. "That'll be the way of it, for sure. Here. Come with me. You can stay at my house, and we'll be away early in the morn that way. Get the others."

That last proved no easy job, as most of the crew was just getting started on the *uisgebeatha,* and finally we left Eachann there, drinking and arguing with a red-headed MacLean, and Gillecolm flirting with a dark-haired MacDonald girl. They both absentmindedly agreed to meet us at the causeway at first light. I doubted whether either of them would sleep this night, but for myself, I was ready to.

The Beaton, as the MacDonald's physician, had a small house just on the mainland, past the causeway, close to the houses of His Lordship's bodyguard.

I stumbled once on the slippery stones of the causeway, and he looked at me sharply but said nothing, not asking how I had come by my limp.

We reached his house and he said, before opening the door, "I'll just be calling out to Mariota, my daughter, to apprise her of the fine guests I've brought with me from the feast at the hall."

This brought a snort of laughter from Seamus, who had drunk a little too much of the claret, what with his father not present to watch over him at the feasting.

I didn't care. I just wanted to sleep. From dawn, when Seamus had first wakened me, until now seemed a lifetime and more. And so I did not look too hard at Mariota as she bustled about in the Beaton's tidy whitewashed house, putting more bedding down by the fire, but merely sat idly, yawning. Finally I lay down on some soft linen-covered mattress—stuffed with heather and bracken I'm sure it was, but not a twig poking me anywhere—and remembered nothing else.

We woke early, too early, I thought, groaning, as we washed and dressed hurriedly in the growing morning light. The cold water helped to wake me, and the hot oatcake with honey and butter did as well. The Beaton served no ale with breakfast, just water, but the thirst was on me after last night's feast and I found that it refreshed me. Seamus had more trouble rousing himself. The strong drink of the night before had gotten the better of him, unused to it as he was. He looked as pale as the sand on the Strand, and only shook his head when the Beaton's daughter offered him a bannock.

"He's taken too much drink," I said to her.

"Fine I can see that," she replied with a little edge to her voice. She went over to the hearth and I watched her uncork some vials and pour some liquid, along with some hot water, in a mazer. She muttered a charm over it while she stirred what was in the cup.

She had a graceful way of moving that was easy to watch, and her long yellow braids hung down as she bent over the fire. I guessed her age to be about twenty, not that much younger than myself. "Here," she said, returning to where we sat, "tell your friend to drink this." She looked at me critically. "And I think you could be using a sip or two of it as well."

"Thank you," I muttered, sounding churlish even to myself.

I handed the cup to Seamus, who downed most of it, making a mouth at the taste of it. He handed it back to me, and I drank the last few swallows. It tasted bitter and dark, but something in it did me some good. After a minute I was noticing I felt more alert, and that Seamus did not look so green and actually was eating his oatcakes.

At this point the Beaton entered the house, looking wide-awake for all the early hour.

"Let's be away, then," he commanded, and we gathered our belongings and made to leave. I was surprised to see his daughter also put on her *brat*, blue it was, I remember, and striped with green, and then gather some things together in a satchel.

"Is she coming with us?" I demanded. She shot me a look for she had heard me. Her eyes were blue, like her father's.

"Aye, and whyever not? We've no patients to see to here, and Mariota has a good eye, and a good mind as well. She serves as my assistant," explained her father, and we left the house.

We met Eachann and Gillecolm at the causeway, along with last night's harper, wanting a ride to Colonsay. Gillecolm had a fine smile on his face but said little of the reason for it.

Yesterday's drizzle had blown away with the night and the sky was crisp blue with fine tendrils of clouds caressing it. The sweet scent of the wild flowers filled my nose and for a moment, as Mariota passed, I smelled a sweeter scent, of elder-flower mixed with something else I could not place.

CHAPTER 3

The Beaton replaced the sheet covering my father's battered face. I looked at him demandingly, but his eyes gave no clue to what the body had told him. Some herbs burning in a brazier, there in the stone room off the infirmary, filled the air with a sharp smoky fragrance. They almost covered the scent of decay which emanated like incense from the body on the plank table, while light from the open doorway and a window high in the wall had picked out the details of my father's injuries rather more clearly than I would have liked.

"And what were you seeing?" I finally asked the doctor.

"The blow to his head was not what killed him," the Beaton replied.

"No?" I was puzzled. I had assumed that great blow to the back of the head had been my father's death stroke. "What was it then?"

Before he could answer his daughter interrupted.

"Did you no see the fine line on his throat? He was strangled with something."

The Beaton again removed the sheet, the better to show me the mark. I saw it again, a faint impression around the neck, partially obscured by the pecking of the gulls and the marks of abrasions and blows. I had not understood the meaning of that sign the first time I had viewed my father's corpse, as shocking as the sight of it all had been to me.

The Beaton gently held open the lid of the one of my father's eyes that the gulls had not pecked at.

"Are you seeing those tiny flecks of blood in the whites of his eyes? And these here, on his face?" the Beaton asked me. "I have seen that before, when men are strangled. The humors explode in the small vessels."

I swallowed.

"And then the bluish tinge to the face. That also is a sign of strangulation. The bloody humors do not return to the heart in these cases, but rest in the head."

"What do you think made the mark?" I asked after a moment. "What did they use to kill him?"

"A fishing line perhaps. A bow string? Any cord would have done it," replied the Beaton to my question. "They stunned him, first, and then wrapped the line about his neck. But they did not leave the line around his neck for long. That is why, perhaps, you did not recognize what it meant at the first. It is much deeper when a man dies from hanging."

He looked at me. "It would have been quick," he said. "Your father did not suffer for long."

"But then why choke him, as well, with the sand?" asked Mariota, with what I thought a decidedly unfeminine interest in the gruesome subject. "The man would have been dead enough by then, what with the blow to his head and all that."

I shuddered, and must have gone pale. She saw me.

"I'm sorry," she apologized after a minute, in a more subdued voice. "It's your father we're speaking of."

I muttered something, I cannot remember what exactly. The Beaton replaced the linen again over my father's corpse, and I told Brother Aidan it could now be readied for the burial Mass.

We prepared to leave. It was time for me to be about my business, or rather the MacDonald's and Gillespic's business, which had in some confused way become mine. I had to find my father's murderer.

I left the Beaton and his out-spoken daughter at the Priory; the *birlinn* would take them on to Scalasaig, as they were to stay a day or so with my uncle at Dun Evin. We would put the story out that they were here to see to any island folk needing a physician, but I felt sure their part in my own inquiries would quickly become common knowledge on Colonsay.

For myself, I set out to find Alasdair Beag.

True to his name, Alasdair Beag was not a tall man, bent short and wizened. He lived alone in a hut on Oronsay close to the Strand, and fished for oysters, clams, limpets and whelks. Most went to the canons, but he sold a few to the masons at their village on Oronsay as well. The story was that he had once been a lay servant at the Priory, but many years ago had moved to his solitary hut hidden among the rocks, where he watched the tides come and go and searched for his shellfish. As he had been the one to find my father's body, it seemed the logical place to start.

I found him sitting outside his small stone hut mending a net.

"Oh, and it is Muirteach," he greeted me. "I was thinking I would be seeing you. The canons themselves were telling me the MacPhee had been sending you to Finlaggan."

So there was no need to explain myself.

"Well, so, you were finding my father, were you Alasdair?"

The old man squinted up at me, and answered matter of factly. "Yes, just as the sky was getting light it was that I found him. The tide had been in, but was going out when I found him lying there."

"And his hand touching the great cross there?"

"Indeed." He bent and worked on his net a minute. "But I am thinking that the water had moved him a bit. Perhaps he did not touch it as he died."

"And were you seeing anything else? A cord there, like a fishing line, or the rock he'd been struck with?"

The old man thought a minute. "Aye," he said, considering. "There was a rock there, by him. A big one that the tide could not be moving so easily. And there are not so many rocks there in the middle of the Strand, so perhaps that is what they used for striking him."

I nodded in agreement. "I will look for the rock. Is it still there?"

"I am thinking it will be there. But the water will have washed it clean. So His Lordship himself is wanting you to find the killer?"

I said that that was true and Alasdair beamed. Then nothing would do but that I tell him something of His Lordship's castle at Finlaggan. The old man listened, rapt. "Well now, that is a fine thing indeed I am thinking, you working for His Lordship," he finally pronounced. "I was not thinking you would ever amount to that much."

It did not seem so fine a thing to me. I wished that the whole affair was over and done with, and myself back in my house at Scalasaig. "You were not seeing anyone unusual that night?" I asked. "Or hearing anything?"

The old man shook his head. "No, just that Tormod, from the masons' village. He is always down by the Strand, after his work is done. He will be taking that old coracle, if the tide is in, or walking if the water is out, over to the coast. I am guessing that Tormod is a fine one for the fishing. So he was there, earlier that evening. I am certain it was him, for I recognized that old plaid cloak he is always wearing, green and brown it is, with a pattern of wide stripes. But that was before the Prior would have gone to Sheena's."

"Did you see Tormod come back that evening?"

"I did not see him, Muirteach, but I ate early and fell asleep. My back pained me that day."

"And my father? Did you see him?"

"I was asleep, as I just told you, Muirteach. But he would have gone to her after Compline. He would stay with her, and then return to the Priory by Matins. That was his way."

My father had installed his mistress, Sheena, in a fine hut across the Strand, near Port a'Chapuill on Colonsay. It was far enough away from the Priory not to cause much comment but close enough that he could see her when time permitted with no great bother. A practical man, my father had been.

I walked the track leading to the Strand, glad for the chance to be alone. The tide was out, and little rivulets of water ran among the sands and seaweed that divided Oronsay from Colonsay. I started across, the sands cold on my bare feet, and passed the large cross, where my father had died. It stood closer to the Colonsay shore, water lines marking its carved stone surface. A bit of seaweed dangled forlornly from one of the arms and of a sudden I felt a lump in my throat. I swallowed it and looked around, seeking the rock Alasdair had spoken of.

There, close by, lay the large black stone, sharp and heavy enough to have been used as a weapon. Alasdair had not lied, the water of the tides had washed it clean and I saw nothing on its wet and glistening surface that told me who had wielded it on my father. But I took it out of the sand and with me to the shore.

When I reached the shore I hid the rock in a place I could find again, and walked the short distance over the rocks towards Sheena's hut.

Sheena had been my father's mistress for some years, an island girl, with family and brothers here as well. We knew each other slightly, although I avoided her as much as I could, for her connection to my father, and Sheena kept herself to herself. Her parents had died some years ago, but her brothers I knew somewhat better, from drinking with them, mostly. Angus and

Alasdair, quick to anger they were and they might well have killed Crispinus at some imagined slight to their sister. And, knowing my father, I had no doubt that there had been many such slights, not all imagined.

Sheena's hut sat tucked in amongst some hills overlooking the sand, not a prepossessing location I thought at first, but as I neared the place and turned to look out towards Islay and Jura, I saw the place had a fine enough view for all that. The sound of a baby wailing fretfully from inside carried outside, and I saw two young children, my half brother and sister, no less, playing like dirty puppies among the black rocks. They stopped and stared at me as I approached their doorway.

"Maire, come here," called their mother from inside.

"But ma, there's a man come—" interjected the boy.

At this Sheena emerged, blinking a little in the daylight after the dark of the hut's interior, carrying her baby, still crying, on her hip. She was a handsome enough woman, with a fine well-rounded figure, somewhat worn now with childbearing and child tending. Sheena was tall, and her reddish-gold hair caught the sunlight, glinting like bronze. Her clothing looked nothing too fine, and nothing too neat as well this morning, a simple kirtle, of greenish wool, and a woolen mantle, woven in plaid design, thrown on against the wind.

It seemed my fine father had done little to ease the life of his handfasted wife. Her skin was tan from being outside, but I could see under the tan a darker bruise on one cheek. Her blue eyes looked swollen and red, and I guessed she herself had been crying along with the bairn.

"Oh, it is yourself," she said, motioning me to sit on the low rock wall which surrounded the cottage. "Would you be wanting a drink, then?"

I nodded.

"Here, watch him for me. Mind he does not get into the

41

muck heap." And with that she deposited her youngest child at my feet and re-entered her cottage.

I looked at my youngest half brother, whose nose ran as he looked back at me. He opened his mouth and I feared he was about to wail again. Sean and Maire, surveying me silently, from a far corner of the yard, offered no help. The babe drew in a deep breath, gathering his wind, as it were, for his battle cry, and I grew desperate and gestured to his sister across the yard.

"Maire, that is your name, is it not? He is about to cry again. Will you no tend him? It's little I know of wee bairns, and I must speak with your mother."

The girl nodded solemnly and came closer, and I breathed a sigh of relief as the little one turned his head to watch his sister.

"Mother says you are our brother," the lass asked, looking at me with gray eyes, which looked suspiciously like my own. "Is that true?"

"Aye," I said, flushing uncomfortably under her direct stare. "It is true, for we have the same father."

"And he is dead now," she said in a curiously flat tone, as she bent and wiped off the snot running from her brother's nose with her hand.

At this point Sheena re-emerged from the hut, her plaid somewhat more tidily wrapped around her, and pinned with a large ring brooch of silver, richly incised with a design of soaring birds and studded with smoky crystal. I guessed the pin must have been a gift from my father. Her hair was braided neatly and she carried a wooden *mether* full of ale.

Sure, it was easy enough to see what it was that had drawn my father to her. The glance she gave me as she handed me the ale had an odd measuring look to it, with a challenge in it that made me uncomfortable, even as I had to admit it somewhat attracted me.

"So you have heard," I said, as I took a long swallow of the drink she offered, despite the sour taste of the ale, then handed the cup back to her. I watched her as she drank deeply, gulping down the ale before she sat down on the wall nearby and answered me.

"Aye, I've heard. My brother came with the news yesterday morning."

"Angus, or Alasdair?"

"Neither. Columbanus."

"Columbanus?" I must have looked as confused as I felt.

Her laughter had a mocking tone to it. "You did not know."

I shook my head, feeling shamed by her amusement.

"Brother Columbanus, you would know him by," she continued. "Did you not know he was my brother also? He was sent to the Priory years ago, as a boy. That one"—she nodded towards the baby—"is named for him. He brought the news yesterday, mid-morning it was when he came here and told me of it."

I felt foolish, then, for not knowing that, but Columbanus had always been at the Priory, and it had never occurred to me to ask about his family, or wonder about it. He had danced perpetual attendance on my father, and that fact alone had made me avoid him the years I had lived there.

"And you have not seen him?"

"Who? Columbanus? Was I not just saying he was here?"

"No. Crispinus. You have not seen the body?"

"How can I go there? You of all people should know I cannot go." Her voice held a sharpness in it, and she shuddered. "Nor do I wish to, perhaps."

It was true. The Prior's mistress could not go to the Priory to see the body of her lover lying in state, prayed over by all the canons as a holy man, despite the whole island knowing of the relationship.

"And are you knowing the rest of it?" I asked.

43

"What? Oh, that you are to find the killer. Aye, I was hearing that as well."

"From Columbanus?"

She shrugged her shoulders and wrapped her plaid around herself more tightly against the wind. "Perhaps." She stood, turned away from me, and picked up the baby, who was crawling toward the midden. "Well, I know nothing to help you."

"You were not seeing him that night? The night he died?"

"Oh, he came. After Compline, as was his habit. But he left here, hale and well alive, long before Matins."

"And was he giving you that bruise on your cheek?"

She turned back towards me suddenly, gesturing towards her cheek. "Och, this? What if he was? For all that, I did not kill him."

"What of your brothers?"

"Who? Columbanus?" She laughed again, a bitter sound in the wind. "Or Angus and Alasdair?"

"Any of them."

"Angus and Alasdair were hunting on Jura. They were gone all the day before, and that night, and were not coming back until the afternoon, yesterday. They caught a fine deer," she added, her chin jutting out a bit in defiance. "They were just giving me some of the venison. Stop by their place and ask them. Perhaps they'll feed you with it."

"And Columbanus?"

"He would not be hurting Crispinus. Never." It was the first time I had heard her say my father's name, and I wondered at the sureness in her voice.

"How do you know that, Sheena?"

"He is a man of God," she said flatly.

"And so was my father, and your lover, a man of God, Sheena," I said, angry now. "And did that keep him from giving you that bruise on your cheek? Did he treat you with honor,

Sheena? And did he treat my mother with honor, for all that he was a man of God?"

She looked at me, and sighed, a long, tired, cold sigh into the wind, a sigh that cut to the bone.

"It's little enough you know of it all, Muirteach, and little enough you know of your father, for all that."

"I know more than enough of him," I replied. "But I do not know who killed him."

She picked up the *mether* with her free hand, settling the child against her hip again. "Mayhap I will go to the burial Mass. Surely they will not begrudge me that. When is it to be?"

"Friday. They are wanting the time for the great lords to arrive."

"Friday is it then," she mused. "Well then, we shall see." And with that she turned and went back inside, leaving me sitting in the wind.

In the end, I took Sheena's advice and stopped at her brothers' cottage. It was not too far from her own, close to Baleromin-more and the beach at Rubha Dubh. Cows had wandered from the byre and munched on the thatching of the roof. The midden heap looked fair overflowing, and, nearby, some dogs fought over a scrap of something. The place showed none of the marks of good order or husbandry that a well-run holding would show. Angus and Alasdair were bachelors, and I felt right at home.

I approached the door, raised the door-flap, and stuck my head inside. All seemed quiet enough. As my eyes adjusted to the dark I began to see the details—the hearth fire out, the ashes cold, I found, when I went to check. Angus and Alasdair were nowhere to be seen.

"Angus! Alasdair!"

Of course they did not answer. Either they had not returned home after visiting Sheena, or they had left again. As I emerged, blinking at the daylight, I heard a noise and got a glimpse of what the dogs were fighting for—a foreleg of a deer. One of the hounds had the hoof in his mouth, and the other, a young puppy, circled, whining, waiting his chance to try and grab it from the larger dog. Or perhaps he just waited for the leavings.

So it seemed Angus and Alasdair had returned home, and left again—to Scalasaig? I was nothing loathe to look for them there, as I felt more than ready to return home myself, and thought longingly of the fire I could build and what I could drink once I returned home. So I hiked the few miles back to Scalasaig, as the winds blew away all the fine weather and a wet drizzle set in.

I found Angus and Alasdair at the tavern. It was not a tavern such as you would find in large cities, that I know now, but the wife of Donald Dubh was a fine ale-wife, and people often gathered there to drink the stuff, and leave some coins in return. As his store of coins had grown, Donald had started to buy claret, and distill *uisgebeatha* as well, and so Scalasaig had its own tavern, for all that it was little more than a hut. And inside it, sitting close to the turf fire and already far-gone with drink, I found Angus and Alasdair.

Of course, the talk today was much of the murdered Prior, but the clamor of voices ceased when I walked in the door. I found a seat on a stool by the fire, and asked for some whiskey. Donald's wife brought a wooden *quaich* quickly enough, and I settled back to drink it, enjoying the bite of it on my tongue. After a few sips I spoke to Angus and Alasdair, who were sitting not far from me.

"I was by your house," I said to them, "and saw your dogs are gnawing away at a fine deer leg. Is that the deer you were lifting from Jura?"

Alasdair looked at me for a moment, then cursed. "I told you to tie that leg up," he said to his brother. "And now himself here is telling us that the dogs have got it after all." He then finished glaring at his brother, who made some reply, and turned to glare at me, instead, his broad face and red hair glinting by the fire light. "And so you were visiting us, Muirteach? What was it you were wanting? And how were you finding out about the deer?"

"Easy enough to see," I said, not answering the first question, "with the hide drying on the roof and the dogs gnawing at the hoof there. But your sister was speaking of it, as well."

"You went to see Sheena?" asked Angus.

Well, Angus had good enough reason to be surprised, for I had never been on good terms with his sister, although my father had taken her as mistress long after my own mother had died. Still, I had resented her, as I resented everyone who thought well of my father. Although after seeing the bruise on her cheek, I wondered now how well she had thought of him.

"So how long was it taking you to hunt that fine stag?" I asked, changing the subject.

Both men were happy to talk of that, and they insisted that they had indeed been on Jura, tracking and hunting the deer, at the time when my father had been murdered two nights ago. And from the look of the carcass at their house I had to think they were perhaps not lying.

But deer can be found on Colonsay as well, and how long does it take to shoot one with a lucky arrow?

"That was a nasty bruise your sister had on the one cheek," I said, after a bit. "However was she getting it?"

Alasdair shrugged his shoulders, and Angus answered. "Och, perhaps himself was hitting her again. He'll no be hitting her the now, at least."

"He hit her often then?" I did not remember my father hitting my mother, but then she had died when I was young, and my father had not come to Islay all that often.

47

"Often enough, although she would deny it. A black heart he had, for all that he was a man of God."

The close air in the blackhouse suddenly stifled me. I drained my cup, stood up abruptly, and went out into the rainy afternoon without another word.

CHAPTER 4

Thinking of the bruise on Sheena's cheek and what her brothers had told me put me in mind of the Beatons. They were physicians, after all, and so instead of heading towards my own fine house in Scalasaig I turned my steps up the hill towards Dun Evin. The rain let up as I climbed, but left the track up to the dun wet and slippery. I was breathing hard when I reached the top, and, my leg aching, turned for a moment before entering the walls to look out on the landscape.

Although with the low clouds the view was not so fine as you could be seeing on other days, I could still see to the east the Paps of Jura and the bulk of Islay some miles away across the water. It was not difficult to understand why the old chiefs had chosen this site for their home, as easily defensible as it was.

A pair of Uncle Gillespic's *luchd-tighe* lounged against the stone and wooden defenses, which surrounded the dun, and just then the sun peeked out through the clouds, sending glints reflecting off of their shields and great swords that leaned against the stones of the fortress wall.

"So it is Muirteach, is it?" commented Fergus Mor, with a bit of a smile. I had known him since my childhood days there, in my uncle's hall. Fergus it was who had helped me take my first red deer in the hunt. "And how was it at Donald Dubh's this afternoon?" he asked.

I grinned a little sheepishly, for him having guessed so quickly how I had spent the afternoon, but only replied, "Fine enough."

"We were hearing about the Prior," interjected the other guard, curiosity evident in his voice. He must, of course, have heard of my mission to Islay.

"Aye," said Fergus. "I am that sorry for you Muirteach. The man was your father."

The words were kindly meant, and brought an unexpected lump to my throat. As I thanked Fergus, I noted how gray streaks now mixed with the chestnut in his beard, and felt suddenly old myself, for all that I was only three and twenty.

Once inside the dun I headed towards the great hall, a rectangular building against the south wall. I blinked as I entered, my eyes adjusting to the dark interior and my nose smelling the acrid odor of the peat fire. After a moment I was able to see Uncle Gillespic, and my aunt Euluasaid sitting at the large table, along with Fearchar Beaton and his daughter.

"Och, Muirteach," my uncle greeted me, "it is yourself. And so His Lordship himself was wanting you to be finding the killer." He beamed. "It is just as I was thinking he would do, and a fine thing indeed it will be to see you bring that black-hearted murderer to justice."

I settled down on a bench, not thinking was such a fine thing as my uncle did. My aunt embraced me warmly, and insisted, as I had hoped she would, that I sit down and eat with them. I watched her put more food on the table: good cheese, bannocks, butter, some venison, fresh milk and honey.

The harper who had come with us from Islay to Colonsay sat closer to the hearth, playing a tune. I would have liked to hear the song about the taking of Castle Sween, but the harper had chosen something less martial and more mournful to play this evening, perhaps in deference to my father's death.

I closed my eyes a moment, listening to the familiar bustle, the hum of her voice, and the sad, lilting notes of the harp, wishing myself back a boy again, at home here with my uncle and aunt, with no murders to solve or dead fathers to avenge.

"Och, Muirteach," laughed my aunt Euluasaid, as I opened my eyes and she handed me a bannock, "and are you as tired as all that? You will be spoiling those good looks of yours if you are not resting a bit."

For some reason I could not understand, my aunt believed me to be handsome, and often teased me on it. But I did realize, as I ate the bannock she had given me, that I was exhausted. The climb had wearied my leg, I'd had too much drink at Donald Dubh's, and the last two days had been far from easy. I pushed the image of my father's body away, however, and smiled at her a little as I ate.

"Are you not thinking, Mariota, that he is well-favored, with that dark hair, and those gray eyes of his? Especially when he is smiling?" she continued. "He has a smile that could be charming the angels, does Muirteach, but we see it too seldom." Well and truly embarrassed now, I was grateful that Mariota did not respond, and I prayed she had not heard my aunt, above the general noise in the hall.

"Now, Mariota," my aunt asked a moment or two later, "what would you be using for teething?" My newest cousin was proving somewhat colicky, and none of my aunt's remedies so far had worked to help the bairn.

I listened idly to Mariota describing to my aunt a concoction of *uisgebeatha*, fennel, and milk until Gillespic interrupted my thoughts.

"You went to Sheena's?" he asked.

"Aye."

"And?"

"She claimed to know nothing, but she had a fresh big bruise on her cheek. Angus and Alasdair claim they were away at Jura, and have a deer to prove it."

"Deer run on Colonsay," said my uncle. "Wasn't it Fergus

who saw a large stag and some other deer just up north of the bay last week?"

"They say Rhodri and Malcolm were with them," I continued, "but Rhodri and Malcolm are gone now, to Barra, for word came that Rhodri's great-uncle was taken ill there, and they left this morning. Myself, I do not see how they could have been doing it, if Rhodri and Malcolm were with them, for I am thinking they have no reason to be killing the Prior whatever," I concluded.

"A great pity that is," said Gillespic, and I looked at him, wondering what he meant by that—a pity that Angus and Alasdair might not be our killers, or a pity Rhodri and Malcolm had no reason to murder my father.

"Still, there is the bruise on her cheek you said," added the Beaton, who had been listening intently. "Is Sheena a big woman?"

"Tall enough."

"Tall and strong enough to kill?"

I did not think so. And whyever would she do so now, at any rate, for my father had been beating her, it seemed, as long as he had known her. I said as much to my uncle and the Beaton. The meal ended. The harper stopped his music and began to eat the food my aunt brought to him while the Beaton, Gillespic, Mariota and I went outside the hall, into the courtyard.

"Perhaps I had best be paying a visit to this Sheena," said Mariota abruptly. I had thought she had not heard my conversation with her father and my uncle, but apparently the discussion of cures for the colic had not prevented her from hearing that, at least.

"Whyever for?" I asked.

"Are you not wanting to know how she got the bruises?"

"Aye."

"And she was not telling you, was she? But she might tell

another woman, and a healer at that."

"Were you not going back to Islay?" I said, starting to argue, but her father interrupted.

"Muirteach, His Lordship himself was wanting me to help you a bit. And though I have inspected your father's body, we were not going to be leaving for yet another day or so; your aunt is aye worried about her youngest, although for myself I do not think she need be. But there may well be some others here who would like to see a physician."

I nodded.

"You should know," he added, "that Mariota herself is a fine healer. And she is good with the speaking, and with the listening. She might be having some luck talking with the woman. And what would be making better sense than that you would be sending her to check on Sheena's bruising."

"She's had bruises before," I said, churlishly, "and none to check on them."

"Aye, and the more pity that, then," replied Mariota tartly.

"I am thinking it is not such a bad idea, Muirteach," put in my uncle. "Fine I am knowing that women have their own ways when it comes to the speaking. Your dear aunt was teaching me that when first we were wed. Perhaps Sheena would talk more to a woman. Although Sheena has never been much of one for words," he added.

We moved out of the way of some chickens rooting in the courtyard, as the last of the sunset faded away in the west, and I considered. My next step, I had decided, for lack of any other ideas, must be to go to the Priory. But if Mariota did visit Sheena, and was able to find out more information about why my father had beaten her, well, that could only be of help. Grudgingly, I was forced to admit as much.

"There, that will be fine then, Muirteach," said my uncle. "You can take the small boat, it is easy enough for one person to row, and you can just be dropping Mariota off near Sheena's on your way to the Priory. It would be best to leave early," he added, "with the tides as they are tomorrow."

For myself, I was wishing the Beaton had never brought his daughter with him, for all the opinions she had and all the complications she was causing. I had been hoping to sleep well into the morning the next day.

"Aye," I agreed, my mood and my exhaustion showing on my face. I wanted sleep badly. In fact, I was feeling too tired to walk down the hill to my own house, and intended to spend the night in my uncle's hall. "I will drop you near her dwelling— you can see the way to it easy enough from the shore. You'll not be worried to walk back from there? I've no way of knowing how long I'll be at the Priory."

Mariota gave me a scathing look, but said only that that would suit. My uncle took the Beaton towards the byre, where the horses were stabled, wanting his advice on a sickly colt. I left them and returned to the hall, where I lay down on one of the benches and promptly fell fast asleep.

Early enough the next morning I watched Mariota gather her satchel together, full of jars of salves and small bottles of tinctures, and we left Dun Evin, heading towards the bay at Scalasaig, before the sun had risen high in the east.

I missed my footing on the way down, the path slippery with mud and dew. Mariota glanced at me, but did not speak of my infirmity, for which I found myself to be thankful. I can just remember running as a small boy, before the wasting fever that came and then left me with the twisted leg, a cripple. Now I only run in my dreams.

"There is a well up that way," I said, nodding towards the path that led northward. "A healing well, of Brigit's." It was a poor effort at conversation, but was all I could think of to say to her. Perhaps she did not know of it.

It seemed she knew of it, for she replied, "I have heard of it. I shall visit it, before we leave."

We walked a bit further in silence. She matched her stride to mine, without comment, although I am sure she could have walked a bit faster on her own. She had that scent of elder-flower about her again, that same perfume I had noticed yesterday morning on Islay. It was some feminine potion or cream she used, I guessed.

"You grew up in Islay?" I finally asked, feeling tongue-tied and awkward.

"Aye." Her voice sounded like nothing so much as the silver bells the old stories say tinkled in Rhiannon's hair. "We live most of the time in Balinaby, but have a house at Finlaggan where we stay when His Lordship is wanting us."

"And your mother?"

"She died in the plague."

We had something in common then, for my own mother had died in the plague as well, when I was but five, but for some reason I did not tell Mariota this. Conversation faltered as we approached the harbor and I readied the boat.

The sun was just rising over Jura, across the waters. The day would soon be growing warmer, and as I began to row us around the island and towards the south end of Colonsay, the water and the islands looked all silver and shimmer in the light, what with the sun shining through the clouds. I heard the splash of seals diving into the water as we neared the beach by the path leading to Sheena's, but more seals lay idly on the black rocks and stared curiously at us. I wondered if they were selkies but, whatever, they had their sealskins on this day.

We did not talk much as I rowed. For myself, I was enjoying the morning, although I felt unaccountably shy around Mari-ota. For some reason I resented this a bit, while at the same time I did not want the trip to end. All too soon we rounded the point and neared the channel to Oronsay.

I had brought the boat into the shallow water, pointed out the path up the rocks and was getting ready to beach the craft, but Mariota stopped me, saying there was no need. She hiked up her skirts, showing a fair bit of lovely white legs as she did so, then disembarked, wading the short distance through the shallow water into the shore. I watched her until she gained the shore, waved, and started up the track, her yellow hair glinting pale gold in the morning sun, and the linen of her shift clinging against her wet legs.

I beached the boat near the Priory and shuddered. It was the thought of my father's corpse, lying in state in the chapel, I supposed. Although, truth to tell, I had never liked the Priory, the noise of the constant construction and the feeling I always had of my father looking over my shoulder, judging me, and finding me wanting. I was glad to have left it seven years ago, when it had become apparent I would never make a monk. But the brothers had taught me reading and writing, and I was grateful enough to them for that. The letters I wrote now for Uncle Gillespic earned me a few coins.

And where should I be starting here, then? Columbanus, Sheena's brother, might be the most obvious person to speak with first. At this time of day I guessed he would be tending to his duties in the bake-house, so I headed there. But before I reached it Brother Gillecristus, the sub-prior, saw me, as he left the chapel and headed towards the cloisters.

"Och, Muirteach, it is yourself. And have you come to pay your respects to your poor father?"

Gillecristus's eyes and his long nose were red. He was closer to my father's age than mine, and had been at the Priory as long as I could remember. He was a MacNeill, from Barra. My father's close friend, he stood fair to become the next Prior.

"I did so yesterday," I said, somewhat curtly. "But His Lordship himself is wanting to know who has done this thing, and has appointed me to find out—"

"And surely that is most proper," Gillecristus interjected piously, "you being his son and all that."

I tried to ignore him, and continued on, "I will be needing a chamber, someplace quiet, where I can be speaking with the brothers privately."

"But you are surely not thinking that someone from our community—"

His smugness irritated me. "And whyever not, Brother?" I asked. "I know well enough how holy you all are here. But His Lordship has requested it, for he must have something to tell the King and the Holy Father, and so . . . "

Brother Gillecristus paled, then his nose reddened. His Lordship, John of the Isles, had founded the Priory some twenty years ago here on Oronsay, where before there had only been a small community of culdees. In addition His Lordship funded all the new construction here, which was extensive. It would not do to be angering him, at all.

Gillecristus snapped his mouth tight shut a moment before he answered.

"Very well," he finally agreed, without any more argument. "I shall see what we can be finding you. Perhaps the chapter house, or that old hut to the east . . . "

I let him deal with it, and it was soon enough that I was ensconced in the chapter house, with pen, parchment, and even a candle, although the room was bright enough from the sunbeams, which found their way in through the slit windows. A young novice was assigned to be my messenger and I asked him to fetch me Columbanus. He arrived soon enough, dusting flour off of his habit as he entered the doorway, blinking as his eyes adjusted to the dimmer light inside.

Columbanus looked little enough like his sister, his eyes a paler and more watery blue than hers, and his hair, where his tonsure had grown out a little, a sandy color. His face was softer and rounder than his brothers' or his sister's, and I guessed that he sampled a bit too much of his own baking.

He had been sent to the Priory as a young boy, and had been there when I had arrived as a child. His age was a few years older than mine. It had never occurred to me to wonder about where he had come from, or what his family had been; Columbanus had simply been part of the priory life, a fixture of it.

An image came to me suddenly, of the young Columbanus crying, sniffling in the dormitory when he thought no one could see him. His tears had bothered me, and I had never liked him much, for all that I had often felt like crying myself there. He had seemed to be a great favorite of my father's, when he was younger, and perhaps that was why I had not liked him. For truth to tell, with both of us being young and miserable, you would think that we would have enjoyed each other's company.

But that had all been long ago, and now Columbanus was still a monk, while I was here to question him.

He said little but stood by the doorway, still brushing the flour off his clothing in a nervous way, although I could not see that much of it remained. I felt awkward but, as he did not speak, eventually I did.

"I have been to see your sister."

He started at that, and glanced at me with his watery blue eyes.

"Sheena?"

"Aye, unless you've another I am not knowing of."

"No. She is the only one."

"And with a nasty bruise on her cheek as well. Would you be knowing anything about that?"

"She had it when I went to see her, the morning after—the morning after the Prior was found."

I heard the hesitation in his voice and wondered what it meant. Why did he hesitate to speak of it? Because the Prior was my father? Simply because the dead man had been the leader of this Priory? Or some other reason?

"So you are not knowing how she was hurt?"

"Ask her yourself."

"I did. But she was not telling me."

"Mayhap she walked into a post. Sheena was always clumsy, even as a young lass."

I let that pass, although I was not thinking that she had gotten that bruise by anything other than a fist.

"And so, whatever, that was not my reason for coming here, to ask about your sister and her bruises," I lied. "I must be finding out where everyone was the night Prior Crispinus was murdered. Sheena was saying you were bringing her the news of it aye early that next day. Where were you that night?"

"Where I always am, Muirteach, at Compline and Matins and Lauds. And asleep in the dormitory in between hours. You can ask the others."

"And you are knowing nothing of why anyone would want the Prior dead?"

A shadow passed over Columbanus's face, tightening the softness of his features and twisting them for a moment. "No more than you do yourself," he replied.

"You were not hearing anyone leave the dormitory that night?"

"No."

"And how was it you were getting permission to see Sheena the next morning?"

"I did not ask. I just left."

I nodded to that. A much simpler way, all told, with the Priory in chaos with the murder. No doubt his dough had risen well enough without him there to watch it, for the time it took him to go see his sister and return.

"Did you see the body before you left?"

"Aye."

"And who would be hating him enough to do that?"

"I am not knowing, Muirteach," he said, and I could hear the anger rising in his voice. "Are you? For sure it is you never liked him much, yourself, nor did he treat you so kindly."

My own anger rose to meet his, but I bit my tongue, trying to keep it in check. The quill of my pen splintered against the parchment and it took me some time to sharpen another, while Columbanus remained standing.

"I had not seen my father much lately, Columbanus," I said finally, when I could speak. "Although true enough it is that we did not get on well together. I have been gone from here for some long time, and things may have changed somewhat, in seven years. So it was just wondering, I was, if you knew of any with reason to want him dead."

"Rather ask who did not have reason," muttered Columbanus, under his breath, but I heard him.

"What are you meaning by that?"

"I meant nothing by it," he denied, "just that he was strict here at the monastery."

Despite further questioning Columbanus refused to say more on it and eventually, stymied, I sent him back to his bake-house.

I had no notion whom to speak with next, but then I thought of Brother Donal. I had been close to him in my years here; he was blessed with a heart warm enough for even an angry lad, and a tongue that was difficult to stop, once he started talking. I asked my novice to fetch him for me, from his work in the library.

Donal looked the much same, the hair of his tonsure sticking up in that same disorderly fashion I remembered. His dark, lean face lit with pleasure when he saw me. "Och, Muirteach," he exclaimed, "it is yourself then. I was hearing that His Lordship wanted you to find out who has done this thing."

I wondered again at the speed with which news travels on these islands.

He paused and looked at me closely a moment before his next words. "It's right sorry I am about your father, Muirteach, for all I am knowing he was none so close to you."

"Aye, we were not close, Donal. But I thank you."

"And a sore loss it will be to our community, as well. He gave good enough guidance throughout these years. Although, like all of us, he must have had his sins. Blessed be his soul," he added, crossing himself.

Donal's way of seeing the good in everyone did not blind him to their faults, and to my thinking he would have made a good prior himself. A better one, perhaps, than my father, but Donal preferred his work among the parchment and the books and had no higher ambitions. Donal had taught me my letters, my reading and my writing, and we had grown close in the years I had lived at the Priory.

I let Donal talk, and it was soon enough that I had found out the latest news of the Priory. It always surprises me what a bunch of gossiping fools an isolated community of canons can be. The sacristan, Brother Aidan, had been chastised at a recent chapter meeting for neglecting his duties, as he had fallen asleep and neglected to set out the vestments for Matins. Brother Moloug, who ran the brew-house, had had a disagreement with Brother Padraic, who kept the bees, and one of the masons had gotten into a shouting match with Gillecristus, who had accused them of shoddy and careless work on the new addition to the west range. But at first thought of it, all seemed much as usual, nothing so extreme as would occasion the murder of the Prior.

"Although there was one thing," Donal added. "Gillecristus and your father argued the day before your father died, something over the construction on the new range. I am thinking it was that Gillecristus wanted the head mason removed, saying the man's work was slipshod, and your father did not, seeing as the man was his kin. It is that Calum Glas, from over near Loch Fada, that was who the man was. And then shortly after that one of the scaffolds collapsed and young Tormod was injured. A sad thing, and now they are saying that he will not be holding a hammer or a chisel again soon, as he was badly bruised and some bones in his hand are broken.

"Yes," Donal continued, stroking his chin reflectively, "it was after Gillecristus and your father quarreled, for you must know that Tormod is some kind of nephew to Gillecristus, and he took it hard. It was Gillecristus who got Tormod his place here, with the masons. And his younger brother as well. I am thinking Gillecristus will be blaming the fall on Calum, and blamed it some on your father as well, for not removing him from the work."

"And where is Tormod now?"

"He is with his people, over near Kilchattan."

"And Calum?"

"He works here still. After your father's death, I am thinking Gillecristus will not be so hasty as to remove Calum, seeing as he was kin to your father. Gillecristus feels badly enough about things as it is. He will be missing your father. They were soul friends a long while."

I had heard a little of the matter, in the tavern, just that a young man from Kilchattan had been injured in a fall, but Donal's view of the matter was enlightening. And it seemed I must speak with both Tormod and with Calum before many more days passed by.

"And what of Columbanus?" I asked, after a time. "Were you knowing he is brother to Sheena?"

"Aye, he has always been close to her," answered Donal. "Indeed, he might be having reason to dislike the Prior, for your father did not always treat his sister well. But I do not think murder is in Columbanus's nature."

"Yet Columbanus seemed very angry just now."

"He has not had a happy life here," said Donal. "You would not be knowing it Muirteach, for it was before you came to us, but Columbanus came here as a child, much as you did. At first he did not take to the life here, but I fear he did not have the sense to recognize it and leave us, as you yourself did."

"Columbanus I remember right well. His crying, mostly," I replied. "And it was older he was then; he must have been all of eleven or twelve."

"Still," Donal continued, "he grew accustomed to the life here and has proved a good enough brother, for all that. He bakes a good loaf, for all that he eats too many of them. That is no secret! There are many ways to serve Our Lord, and sure none of us could serve him without bread to eat. And Columbanus bakes well." Donal's smile lightened his lean face.

"But then who has done this?" I asked in frustration, after a moment. "And why was my father killed just touching the cross, as though seeking sanctuary himself?"

"I am not knowing, Muirteach. But I will listen here for you, at the Priory. Perhaps something will come to light." He turned to go, then stopped, turning again to face me. "Now that I am thinking of it, Muirteach, it seems that I heard someone leave the dormitory that night, well before Matins. I woke when I heard the creak of the stairs. I assumed whoever it was had been going to the necessarium, and indeed, so they might have been."

"You did not hear them return?" I asked.

"Forgive an old man, Muirteach," he said. "I fell back to sleep."

"Who sleeps near you in the dormitory?" I asked.

"Well, there is Brother Aidan and then Columbanus, up, away from the stairs. And Padraic, and then Brother Moloug, across the hall."

"I have already spoken with Columbanus, not that he may not have lied to me. So perhaps I should be speaking with Brother Aidan or Padraic the now."

"It is close to time for the meal. Eat with us, and leave it until after."

CHAPTER 5

So it was that I sat in the refectory, with the brothers, and listened to the lector read from the Psalms while I ate the soup, fish, and bread, fresh baked by Columbanus, that made up the canons' midday meal. Although the food was good, the experience put me in mind of my early years there, and I grew restless, glad when the lector finished his reading and the canons stood to leave.

After that, while the majority of the canons studied, I returned to my desk in the chapter house and questioned both Aidan and Padraic. Both flatly denied having left the dormitory that evening, except for the holy offices, and so my thoughts turned again to Columbanus.

Could he not have left the dormitory, knowing my father would most likely be going to see Sheena, and waited for him on the Strand as he returned? It was clear he had not liked Crispinus, both for his sister's sake, which might well be motive enough for murder, and perhaps for his strict rule here at the Priory. His muttered comment and subsequent refusal to clarify it had made me even more suspicious of the man.

Yet Sheena, and more importantly Donal, had both said he could not have committed murder. Sheena would lie to protect her brother. Donal's judgement I trusted, but perhaps he was wrong in this matter.

Perhaps Sheena had killed my father? She was a strong enough woman, but she seemed to gain little by his death, except for an end to beatings, for she now had no protector, and would find life harder than before, with three bairns and no man. I supposed Angus and Alasdair might help her some with that, and I pushed the thought of my hungry half brothers and half sister out of my mind. It would be interesting to hear what Mariota had discovered on her visit to Sheena's.

Or Angus and Alasdair could have done it, and lied about the deer.

However there was still the other matter, of Tormod's fall, and the quarrel between Gillecristus and my father. I reflected that a visit with Calum would be in order, and so I gathered my parchment and pen into my satchel, left the chapter house and wandered over towards the area of new construction. The workmen were cleaning up the worksite, their day's labors almost ended, stacking stones in piles and putting away their tools, and it was easy enough to find Calum Glas. He was a strongly built man, with a hooked nose, dark complected like so many of the MacPhees. The covering of stone dust he wore made it obvious how he had earned his byname; the man did, indeed, have a gray look to him.

I recollected he was kin to me, as his father had been second cousin to my own father and to Gillespic. But I did not know the man well. As a mason he traveled, working on abbeys in Kintyre, Iona, and all throughout the Isles, and seldom was he on Colonsay for long periods of time.

He did not recognize me and I had to introduce myself.

"Och, Muirteach. When last I saw you, you were just a young lad, and in the robes of a novice. You've grown. And what are you doing the now?"

"Little enough," I answered. "Some scriving for Gillespic. Drinking. And now a bit of work for His Lordship himself," I added, for it was soon enough that Calum would hear of it and there was no point in lying. "He is wanting to know who murdered my father and has set me to be finding out."

Calum said nothing and his expression looked less welcoming to me. I pressed on. "They were saying that Gillecristus and Crispinus had argued. Something to do with the construction. Were you hearing any of it?"

"Perhaps I was," he finally admitted. "That Gillecristus is as bitter as the withy stick. He was not wanting me to be working here because I am related to that fool MacIain that slew his own uncle some years back. But he would not be admitting that that was the reason and had to be accusing me of shoddiness in my work. And for that I am thinking that they had words about it, after Gillecristus came here and was accusing me, right in front of all the workmen, bitter old man that he is."

"But then what of the scaffold that collapsed?" I asked. "Was not young Tormod sorely injured?"

"Indeed, and a sad day that was. But I had cautioned the young *amadan* more than once to double-check his scaffolding before he goes up, and was he ever listening to me? He had his brother do it, and his brother is but a lad, just learning the trade, and not to be trusted. Headstrong Tormod is, and now he will be having the twisted hand to prove it. He may even walk with a limp, they were not sure of that last."

He looked at my leg, and caught himself. "Och, I am sorry Muirteach, I was not meaning anything by that."

"But could anyone have wished Tormod harm?" I asked, ignoring Calum's last comment. "Was there anything about the scaffold that was at all suspicious?"

"Nothing," he assured me blandly, "for all that he is none so popular. But no mason would endanger another. You must know, Muirteach, accidents are no so uncommon in this trade." And that, I supposed, was true enough.

The sun was turning towards the west, the bells began to toll for Vespers, and of a sudden it became clear to me that I had

spent enough time at the Priory for one day. I bid good-bye to
Calum and prepared to leave, stopping by the chapel for a
perfunctory prayer by my father's bier and not waiting for the
Mass, which was about to start. Gillecristus, busy with the
service, could not detain me to learn what I had discovered,
and shamefully I felt somewhat relieved at that. I had little of
importance to tell him, and still less that I wanted him to know.

My mind was a jumble of a few facts and many more suppositions and as I sailed the boat around the island back toward
Scalasaig it was little enough I knew what to make of them all.

As I beached the boat I saw Seamus waiting there, with Somerled beside him. He had probably been waiting there all day, I
thought, a little guiltily. I had neglected the lad since our return
from Islay, but perhaps Seamus himself had been needing some
of that time to be feeling to rights again, after his overindulgence
at His Lordship's feast.

My dog, however, raced back and forth, barking wildly as I
approached in the boat, heralding my arrival to the entire port
of Scalasaig. The fishermen unloading their boats showed little
interest in Seamus, my dog or myself.

"So and what were you discovering?" Seamus asked broadly,
as I pulled the boat onto the shore.

I scowled, and shrugged my shoulders. "Sure enough it seems
my father was murdered by the *sithichean,* for I am not knowing
who did this. Come along then, and I shall tell you what I do
know," I added, seeing his disappointed face.

I gathered up my satchel and we started to walk towards my
house. Seamus knew both Tormod and his brother. Seamus's
mother, it turned out, was distantly related to Tormod's mother,
Chatriona. The boys had played together as children, although
Tormod was some four or five years older. Seamus had not seen
Tormod since his accident, and so it was easy enough to ar-
range to visit him along with Seamus tomorrow.

We neared the collection of dwellings that comprised the village of Scalasaig. Seamus's mother, Aorig, met us as we approached the door to my hut.

"You should be feeding that dog, Muirteach. He was after my cheeses that I had just set out to cure in the sun."

"Seamus, did you not feed him?" I asked quickly, trying to shift the blame, but Aorig was not one to be fooled by that. She knew me too well.

"You should not be expecting that Seamus will be feeding him without you leaving him something to give to the poor thing. He has his own chores to be doing, as he well knows, although he is happy enough to forget them when he can."

"Was he getting the cheeses, then?" I asked. Aorig was a good neighbor, and often asked me to share food with herself and her husband, and I was not wanting to inconvenience her.

"No he was not. But it was no thanks to you. I gave the dog some burned porridge and he seemed happy enough to get it. But a big dog like that, he is needing more to eat than burned porridge."

"Well, he should be hunting for it, then."

"It was hunting he was, Muirteach. He was hunting my cheeses, and then my chickens, the big shaggy oaf that he is."

My dog was not fierce. In fact Uncle Gillespic had given him to me in disgust when it became apparent that the big gray deerhound was a pathetic hunter. I had named him Somerled, after the illustrious founder of Clan Donald, but this Somerled much preferred lounging by my fire and scrounging scraps from Aorig to any feats of valor. The bulk of him was warming in the hut, and he was company, of sorts, and never complained about my housekeeping. Aorig had described my dog very well.

"Oh, and I was not telling you Muirteach; I have not seen you. Your uncle came by the day they found your father. It was after you were gone to Islay, that he came."

"What was he wanting?"

Aorig shrugged. "I am not knowing for sure. But he was asking me where you were that night your father died. When I told them I had seen you in your house that night the worse for drink, and I had heard your snoring later, your uncle seemed aye happy, and was saying something about good finally coming out of your drinking. What was he meaning by that?"

So Gillespic had even suspected me. The thought stung like a nettle weal. Although it hurt to think he had suspected me, grudgingly I admitted to myself that perhaps it had been canny of my uncle to make sure I had indeed been at home all that night. I had, after all, had little enough good to say of my father in the past few years.

Just at this point Somerled choose to sound the alarm as one of Aorig's chickens came around the corner, and in the general mayhem that ensued Seamus and I made our escape into my house. We were followed shortly by Somerled who limped in, whining, and settled by the fire, licking his hind leg. Aorig had clouted him, but saved her chicken.

I had just started the fire against the evening chill, and was preparing to tell Seamus of my day, when his mother's white-coifed head poked around the leather flap that served as my doorway.

"Muirteach, there is a woman here looking for you. It is that daughter of the physician, I am thinking. I will be sending her in to you. And Seamus, I am needing you to go fetch the cattle back. And then we will be eating. If you want to join us, Muirteach, you will be welcome. But do not be bringing that dog of yours over at all."

I stood up quickly, oversetting the bucket of water, swore, and turned around, embarrassed by the mess of the hovel I called my house. Mariota stood in the doorway, her forehead wrinkling as her eyes adjusted to the darkness.

"I was just coming back from Sheena's," she said somewhat apologetically, "and thought to stop and tell you what I found."

Her delicate nose wrinkled as she sniffed at the smoky air, which mingled aromatically with the dunghill out back. My fire always smoked, and the thatch, although filled with leaks when it rained, made a fine enough barrier to prevent the smoke escaping.

"May I sit down?" she asked, and I hastily found the three-legged stool, dumped the cloak and dirty bowl that had been sitting on it on the bed, dusted it off and placed it by the fire.

"Here," I said. "I am sorry. I am not used to having women here."

"Fine I can see that," she returned.

"I was just returning from the Priory. Would you be wanting some drink? I've no food to offer you."

"I am not surprised by that," Mariota said tartly, but, to my surprise, she accepted some *uisgebeatha*, after I had found a cup and wiped it out, and settled herself on the stool, gathering her skirts somewhat carefully around her. Somerled roused himself from his place by the hearth to come and lay his large head on her lap.

"A fine big dog you have here," she observed, as she scratched at his ears. Somerled responded to this gesture by trying to climb into her lap.

"How is it you have a deerhound?" Mariota asked, as we tried to convince Somerled to get out of her lap. It was an understandable question, for usually none but the lords owned deerhounds.

"My uncle was giving him to me. The dog took a liking to me and he is a bad hunter."

"So what were you finding at the Priory?" she asked, after Somerled had finally settled back down at Mariota's feet, leaning his bulk against her skirts.

I scowled. "Brother Gillecristus, the sub-prior, swears that no canon could have committed such as act, for all that I am knowing they are as great a bunch of prideful fools as ever walked the earth.

"A young mason fell from a scaffold the day before the murder, and I suppose someone could have held my father to account for it, as Gillecristus and my father argued over the construction shortly before that happened. But Calum Glas, the master mason, says it was an accident only, and no cause for suspicion. No one admits to knowing anything of any use, at all, at all," I finished, in frustration, "but I am not sure I have been asking the right questions.

"Brother Columbanus insists he was in the dormitory, asleep, when the Prior left, but it is clear he has no love for my father. And he is Sheena's brother. I think Columbanus could easily have left, met the Prior when he was returning, and killed him then. Brother Donal said he heard someone leave the dormitory that night."

"Why? For his sister's sake?"

"Indeed, that is the way of it, I am thinking. It was clear he was not liking the Prior, from the little he did say."

"That is possible. And if he cares for his sister, it is plain that the Prior did not treat her well."

"What did you find at Sheena's?"

Mariota settled her skirts about her for a moment before she answered me.

"She is not an easy woman to talk to, Muirteach, but after a while she opened up a bit to me. The wee bairn was peevish with the teething, and so I made a remedy for that, and gave her some wormwood for the bruising, and—"

"Was she saying how she got the bruise?" I interrupted.

"Aye, she was, but you must be waiting for me to tell you. You are not patient, are you Muirteach?" she asked, smiling a wee bit, but then she herself did not wait for my answer. "She told me the Prior hit her, that last night he came."

Well, that was as I had expected, really. "Did she say aught of Columbanus?" I asked.

Mariota laughed. "Muirteach, she knows I am trying to help you. I do not think she would be saying much about Columbanus, even if she did know he had killed your father. He is her baby brother, for all that he is a grown man and a canon."

"And what of herself? She is a strong woman, after all."

Mariota shook her head. "She is truly grieving for him. And his death will mean nothing but trouble for herself and the bairns."

"She could have killed him," I insisted stubbornly, "after he beat her."

"But why at the Strand?"

"So they would not be finding the body back at her cottage, *amadain*."

"Perhaps," said Mariota, but I could tell by the look around her mouth that she was not believing me. "Whoever hit him was tall, and struck him from behind," she added.

"Sheena is tall," I replied, but Mariota did not answer that. "And there are her brothers as well. Perhaps they came, and found him beating her, and then they murdered him. They could have lied about the deer."

Mariota shook her head stubbornly, and I gave it up and tried a different tack. "Why was my father giving her that bruise? You were forgetting to tell me."

"You were not giving me the chance, Muirteach."

"Well, I am giving you the chance now," I said sourly, then wished I could take my words back.

"Did he need a reason? He could have hit her for anything that displeased him. She said he did not have any reason to beat her, but it was a feeling I was having, just, that she was not telling me all she knew of it."

The thought of it sickened me, but I knew my father well enough to know the truth of what Mariota said. My father had hit me, on occasion, as a child, when the temper was on him. Sheena could have done anything, or nothing at all.

"So what is next?" Mariota asked, after a moment.

"Seamus and I will visit Tormod."

"What of other people here on Colonsay?" she asked, after a moment. "Is there no one here who would have wanted the Prior dead? What of Tormod's kin? Would they be blaming your father for his fall?"

"Better to blame Calum Glas. And Calum is strong, but he would not be killing my father. He defended Calum, when Gillecristus wanted him taken off the job."

"What of someone from Islay? They could have beached a boat on the Strand and waited for him, if they knew his habits."

"There is only my mother's kin. And if they were going to kill him, they'd have been doing it eighteen years ago." I thought a moment. "I shall have to return to the Priory." The look on my face gave me away.

"You are not liking it there," Mariota observed. "Why?"

"I spent my boyhood there," I said. I could have said that I hated it there, and had hated my father the most of all, but I did not, and remained silent.

"What of Gillecristus?" Mariota asked. "They argued. He benefits from your father's death, does he not? Is he not likely to become the next Prior?"

"I have never liked him," I admitted. "He is ambitious. But he has known my father for many years; they founded the Priory together twenty years ago. They were close."

"Ambition could, perhaps, drive a man to murder," mused Mariota.

"I shall talk with him again, or perhaps Donal can find out

something more." So then there was no help but to tell her of Donal and how he was keeping his ears open for me, there.

"Your Canon Donal seems a kind man," she said. "So perhaps all was not bad at that place."

I did not answer. After awhile Mariota must have realized I was not going to say anything more, for she set her cup down on the floor, and stood up, brushing the dog hairs off her skirts. "I should be going," she said. "My father will be waiting for me up at the dun."

I stood awkwardly by the door as she left, that scent of elder-flower wafting past me, then I went and filled my cup again with *uisgebeatha*.

The next morning Seamus and I set out early, to walk to Kilchattan where Tormod and his family lived. The morning was foggy. Somerled loped by my side, eager at the chance for the outing, leaving us every few minutes to chase a rabbit, then returning, after a minute or two, without catching any. He was, as I have already said, a lazy dog.

We reached the little settlement of Kilchattan in good time. Tormod's home lay somewhat before the old chapel, still used by the village. The homestead looked in good repair, well kept and tidy, with the thatching of the roof held down by rope netting weighted with rocks. We approached the door-flap and knocked on the stone walls of the house.

An older woman answered our summons, short, round, and neat as her holding, with her hair tidily coifed and wrinkles of worry behind her blue eyes.

"And whoever is it then?" she asked. "Och, it will be you, Seamus. It is good to be seeing you—how you have grown tall! And how is your mother faring?"

Seamus replied Aorig was well, and gave Tormod's mother the cheese that Aorig had sent. Chatriona told us her elder son was recovering, but still weak, and would be glad of our company for some short time as she ushered us inside.

Some time was taken up with pleasantries while Chatriona settled us with some mead and bannocks by Tormod, and then took her spinning outside while we visited with her son. The lad lay propped up against the wall on his bed, a pile of bracken covered with blankets, in a corner of the cottage. One arm rested awkwardly on his blanket, and from the looks of the bandaged hand, with purplish bruises fading to yellow and green visible outside the bandages, he would have a hard time carving again. His face looked pale, as thin and angular as his mother's was round, with a sour and a fretful look to it.

"I was hearing of your accident, Tormod," said Seamus, after we had greeted him, "and was just wondering how you were doing with it all. A sad thing indeed, to be hearing of it."

Tormod grimaced. "Aye, a foolish thing it was."

"How did the accident happen?" I asked.

"The scaffolding collapsed. I am not knowing how or why, as I had Eogain check it before I went up."

"Eogain?" I asked.

"That is Tormod's wee brother," interjected Seamus. "So he is working there as well?"

Tormod nodded. "Aye. He is just fetching stones and the like now. But I had him check the scaffold. There looked to be nothing wrong with it. Calum Glas was the one who supervised the making of it. The master mason." Tormod spat out these last words.

"What are you saying Tormod?"

He turned his head wearily. "Just that himself is always too busy, hurrying to get things done to the satisfaction of that Prior, to be looking to the safety of his scaffolding. He curries favor, does that man. I will not work for him again."

Whether Tormod meant that he would refuse to work for

Calum or that he would not be able to work again I was not sure.

"But surely he would see to the safety of his men?"

Tormod shrugged and said nothing. I tried again. "Are you saying he would not?"

"Och, I do not know. Fine he is always making up to Prior Crispinus, and lashing us with his tongue to work faster, so how would I be having the time to check that scaffolding before I am climbing up it?"

Which could mean anything. After puzzling on it for a moment I decided Tormod must have meant that was the reason his brother had checked it.

"Were you knowing that the Prior and Gillecristus were arguing? Gillecristus was wanting Calum taken off the job."

"That dried up old stick of a man!" Tormod scowled, which I noticed he did frequently. It was not a pleasant expression. "I am guessing who won that argument. I would not like to be crossing that Crispinus."

"Why not?"

Tormod thought a moment before he answered. Finally he replied, "He is a man who will always be getting whatever it is that he is wanting, no matter what it is that is in his way."

I had to agree with that assessment of my father. I changed the subject, saying nothing about my own relationship to Crispinus. Evidently Tormod had not heard of the Prior's bastard son and I saw no reason to enlighten him.

"Were you knowing," Tormod continued, "that Crispinus was always after the masons, even after the boys who carried the stones, berating them, telling them to work harder. As though it was his business."

I shook my head. "I was not knowing that. Did he do so to you?"

"Perhaps."

"Gillecristus is kin with you, is he not?"

"Aye, on my mother's side."

"But you were not hearing about the Prior?"

Tormod's eyes narrowed in a way I found I did not like. "What about him?" he asked.

"He was found murdered on the Strand. Three days ago now, it was."

Tormod turned his head away a moment before he looked at us again. "The black heart of him. Well, he will not be bothering the workers anymore. Or anyone else, either."

He took a drink from the cup sitting near on a stool near his bed, his face pale. "I had not heard of it," he added. "I have had a fever. Mayhap my mother knows of it."

"I would think young Eogain would have brought word."

"We have not seen him since I was brought home. He will be staying at the masons' village there on Oronsay."

"But how are your injuries? Will you be working again?"

"I am not knowing. They say my hand was broken in some three places, and there is a sore pain in my back, but I can move my legs so perhaps, once the bruising heals . . . they are thinking it is only a bad sprain of the legs and the back. At least I should still have the strength in my arms and shoulders for carving the stone, but I am not knowing if I will be able to hold the chisel."

It was just at this point that Chatriona returned. She took one look at her elder son's white face and sent us on our way, telling us that himself would be wearing himself out now, with his visitors, and we must be off with him just getting over the fever and needing rest to heal from his injuries.

It occurred to me that perhaps the Beaton could be of some use, and I offered to send him to look at Tormod's injuries, for which his mother thanked me. Tormod however, just sat staring at the thatching while we said our good-byes to his mother, and did not respond to our farewells.

"You've fair worn him out, the white love," she said, firmly showing us the door. "Give Aorig this honeycomb, and thank her for the fine cheese, Seamus. We will be enjoying it, along with her kindness." And with that we left.

"It is plain to see that Tormod could not have killed your father," said Seamus when we were some half-mile down the track leading back to Scalasaig. "With him being in bed and not able to walk and with the fever and all."

I remembered, then, how Alasdair Beag claimed to have seen Tormod on the Strand the evening my father died.

"Aye," I agreed, "unless he is lying about his injuries. And what man here does not have kin to avenge him?"

CHAPTER 6

The voices of the monks echoed around me. I stood in the Oronsay Chapel, that next day, as they chanted the funeral Mass of my father. The scent of frankincense almost covered the odor of decay emanating from the linen-shrouded corpse, covered with an embroidered pall, which sat on a bier before the altar. Beeswax candles flickered in the chapel, their scent adding to the perfume in the air, the light from the flames glinting on the chased silver of the sacramental vessels.

My father's funeral. What was I feeling then, as the visiting bishop from Iona consigned my father to the earth?

I told myself I felt little grief, and concentrated instead on my problem. Who among these people had wished my father dead? Or, I thought, remembering Columbanus's mutterings, who had not?

I stood in the crowded chapel, Seamus next to me, and watched the other mourners. Gillecristus, at the altar, assisted the Abbot of the Isles, who had come from Iona to officiate, with the Mass. His head lowered, he looked suitably pious and had I not disliked the sub-prior so much I would have said he looked grief-stricken.

The Lord of the Isles stood in the front of the new chapel that he himself had endowed, and I thought I saw some satisfaction on his features as he surveyed the fruits of his generosity.

His Lordship had dressed finely, in a garment of silk, although the cut of it mimicked a man's linen great-shirt. A large gold brooch set with a ruby pinned his rich mantle, which was of finely woven wool but had a richly embroidered satin lining to it. His older son Ranald, the one he had gotten on Amie MacRuarie before he put her aside to marry Margaret Steward, stood slightly behind him, along with the two of his sons from Margaret not hostage with the King in Edinburgh.

He himself had made my father Prior, and my father had been known as His Lordship's man. Surely His Lordship had no reason to have my father killed.

The other great chiefs of the Isles had voyaged to attend the funeral as well, the MacLeans from Lochbuoy and Duart, the MacNeills of Barra and Gigha, the MacKay and the MacGillivray from Mull, and the MacNicoll from Portree, along with their many retainers. All made a brave show in their embroidered saffron *léines* or great-shirts, covered with finely woven *brats,* which were pinned proudly with great brooches of silver, and even some of gold, set with fine gemstones and gleaming in the candlelight from the altar.

But as little as I knew of my father's dealings with these chiefs, I did not think murder on the Strand would be their way of killing a churchman who had angered them. More like it would be a sword in the chapel, as the English had killed Saint Thomas.

Farther back in the chapel stood the masons, Calum Glas among them. I looked for signs of guilt on his face, but saw none, just his sharp eyes surveying the scene. My three half siblings, with Sheena, her head covered by her plaid, stood alongside my aunt Euluasaid and some of my cousins. Angus and Alasdair stood there as well, escorts to their sister, along with other folk who had traveled from the large island to attend.

Sheena, Brother Donal told me later, had asked no one's leave, but had simply arrived at the service, although Brother Gillecristus had declared in the chapter meeting the previous day that he would not tolerate that whore coming to the Mass. Apparently this had not been heard by Brother Columbanus, or had been deliberately disobeyed, and Sheena, ignoring the glares of Gillecristus, had entered the church, flanked with Angus and Alasdair for her *luchd-tighe*.

They had arrived as the bishop began to say the Mass, at the last possible moment. Columbanus had hurried to his sister, kissing her on the cheek, and showing her a place to stand in the back of the chapel, and so it was that she was there. And I found myself thinking that I would not like to be in Columbanus's place, when Gillecristus became the next Prior of Oronsay.

Also Mariota and her father stood in the chapel, but I forced my thoughts away from them as I listened to the Mass. I tried to think of my father and his immortal soul, then tried to focus on the service, and then tried, yet again, to ponder who the killer might be, but it was soon enough that, for all my efforts at thinking, the Mass was over. The body of my father was deposited in its crypt in the church, the last wails of the keening women fell away, and we all filed out into the sunlit afternoon.

I spied Mariota speaking with Sheena as we left the church. Sheena's eyes were red, her face blotchy with grief, and her expression stoic. After a moment's conversation with Mariota she turned and started walking back over the hills towards the Strand and her home, her children trailing behind her.

I had not yet spoken with His Lordship about my researches, and had no chance to do so as we filed into the refectory for the funeral feast. I looked for Mariota. I told myself I wanted to ask her about her conversation with Sheena, but she was already sitting with her father next to some of the Islay MacDonalds. So I sat between Seamus, and Angus and Alasdair, who had not left with their sister.

I tried again to ask them about the deer, but they stuck stubbornly to their story, insisting Rhodri and Malcolm would vouch for them when they returned from Barra. They were friendly enough to me, for all my questioning, and did not seem consumed by guilt, eating heartily of their brother's fine bread and the rest of the funeral feast. Perhaps, I thought sourly, they were happy to see my father in his grave.

The food tasted good. Gillecristus and the other canons put on a great spread for the honored guests, for it was not every day that the Abbot of the Isles himself, as well as His Lordship and all the other great chiefs, came to the Priory. It was my guess, however, that the canons themselves enjoyed the beef in cameline sauce, frumenty, venison, and the other meats and delicacies served that day.

In deference to the religious setting, the bards played only songs glorifying Our Lord, and songs of the more secular type were not performed, although some praises of the late Prior were performed. The feast broke up by late afternoon and the lords prepared to depart.

I spoke with the Lord of the Isles as he walked down to the beach, now crowded with all the galleys of the chiefs. It was hard enough, what with all the clamor of leave-takings, to find a place to speak privately, but we walked a little down the shore and towards the black rocks in the west. The clouds stretched out over the sea towards Ireland, wisps of white against the blue of the sky. Gulls wheeled overhead, crying their short, sharp cries while I told His Lordship the little I had learned so far, my suspicions of Angus and Alasdair, of their sister, of Columbanus, of Gillecristus's and Crispinus's argument over the construction, and of Tormod's injury.

His Lordship listened gravely enough to my suppositions, his eyes alert.

"So you are thinking it is one of the masons, then?" he asked, walking with me back towards the *birlinns* whilst his crew readied his galley. "Or perhaps his woman that did it, along with her brothers?"

I confessed, my heart pounding, that I did not yet know for sure, and waited upon his displeasure. His Lordship frowned a bit, but then after a moment only clapped me on the back, with what seemed to me a somewhat false heartiness.

"Sure, and we must be solving this, Muirteach, and that right soon. Already the Abbot at Kintyre has been asking me of it, saying that he will be writing to the Holy Father. Let alone that the King will be wanting it solved quickly enough, and we cannot be giving him an excuse to be bothering himself with these parts, as you well know."

To tell the truth it was little enough I knew of the moils of politics. Up until my father's murder I had spent the majority of my days drunk either at my house, or at Donald Dubh's. Still, it did not take a wise man to know that His Lordship would not be wanting King Robert to be sticking his nose into the business of the Isles, and so I said nothing, nodding my head in what I hoped His Lordship would take to be sage agreement.

"So you see, Muirteach," His Lordship continued, "you must be finding the murderer, and that right quickly. Or you must be finding someone you think could well have done the murder. Aye, that would do almost as well, I am thinking. Are you understanding what I am saying?"

I felt a sick griping in my guts. I understood well enough. Either I must find the murderer or I must find a scapegoat for the murder of my father.

"You are not saying I must accuse an innocent person of his murder?" I dared to ask. I heard my blood throb in my ears as I waited for his answer.

His Lordship's face clouded a moment.

"No, now, Muirteach, I could never be saying that. What would be the justice in that? The murder-price must be paid, and things set back to rights. I am saying that the murderer must be found, that is all. And," His Lordship added, almost as an afterthought, as he turned to rejoin his retainers, "t'would be best if it were not one of the canons."

I watched him stride away, and onto his galley, followed by his sons, other retainers, and his harper. The galley pulled away towards Islay, and I kicked at the sands of the beach in frustration before Seamus and I boarded my uncle's galley for the short trip back to Scalasaig.

There was more food and drink at my uncle's. It appeared Mariota and her father would be staying on Colonsay a bit longer. There were many on the island eager to call on the Beaton, such was his great fame as a physician, while Mariota had agreed to use her considerable expertise in helping my aunt put up some cordials and other remedies. I did not doubt they would be busy during their time here.

Over a glass of claret, the Beaton professed himself curious to visit Tormod, and wondered if his injuries were in fact as severe as the man claimed them to be, especially when I told him Alasdair Beag claimed to have seen him that same evening.

"And I will be keeping my ears and eyes open as well, Muirteach, in case I am hearing anything to help you." Mariota's blue eyes had a glint in them as she spoke that irked me, and I fear I spoke harshly in reply.

"Such as what?"

Her chin moved outwards a fraction. "Such as who was beating Sheena that night."

"Was it not my father?"

"I am wondering, now, if it might have been someone else entirely. She spoke with me after the funeral Mass."

I remembered seeing the two women speaking, after the Mass, but had not yet had a chance to ask Mariota about it. It irritated me that she had mentioned it before I had asked her about it.

"And?"

Mariota caught at her lower lip with her small white teeth, and thought a moment.

"She seemed aye remorseful, Muirteach," she said finally.

"Aye, perhaps she is remorseful because she killed my father. Along with those brothers of hers."

Mariota shook her head. "No, Muirteach. She seemed afraid as well. Although I do not believe she killed your father, I am thinking she knows something of it. She kept looking behind her, as though she did not want someone to see her speaking with me, but I am not knowing who that would have been."

"Her brothers more than likely," I answered.

"She asked me for more teething lotion for the bairn, so perhaps she will tell me more when I see her."

"And is there aught else?" I asked, for it seemed, from her look, that Mariota had more to say.

"It was something I saw her wearing at the funeral. A man's pin, a large and fine one, which did not look as though it had belonged to a prior. She had it on her plaid."

I remembered that as well. The pin she had worn when I had gone to see her at her cottage on the day my father had been killed.

"I have seen it," I replied. "Large, is it not? Silver, with a pattern of birds and a fine cairngorm on it?"

Mariota nodded.

"I am thinking my father must have given it to her."

"Perhaps," said Mariota, but although I felt she was unconvinced we spoke no more of it.

I drank too deeply that night, up at Dun Evin, listening to the songs of the bard, and my uncle telling stories of my father from his youth, as a way of mourning him. I had never known that he had had a puppy as a child, named of all most ridiculous things, *Coinean,* a rabbit, and for some reason the thought made me maudlin. I tried not to cry, but in that perhaps I was not altogether successful, and somehow stumbled down the hill to my hut to sleep much later that night.

All too soon there was more trouble. Had I been knowing that was going to be the way of it, perhaps I would not have been drinking as much as I did that night.

That night I dreamed of my father. Wrapped in his death-shirt, he stood in front of my bed and looked at me accusingly, the windings of his grave-clothes flapping in some ghastly faerie breeze. I could see the bruises on his throat, and the mark of the string that had throttled him. All around him fey candles burned with a ghostly, glimmering light, the green flames flickering in that same silent unearthly wind, at times lit by flashes of a greater light, like some hellish lightning.

"Muirteach," he called to me in a hollow voice. "Muirteach."

"What is it, Father?" I answered in my dream. "Are you not dead? We buried you today, a fine funeral Mass. How is it you are speaking with me?"

"Och, Muirteach, yes, I saw. Were you thinking I was not there? It was a fine funeral indeed, and it is dead indeed I am. A sad undignified death it was, too. Little did I think that I, the Prior of Oronsay, would die in such a sad way. It was a fool I was to think that I could avoid my fate."

And then my father started to quote the bards, and it was this that made me believe it was a true vision and not just the whiskey talking to me.

" 'Carry not to the house of the spotless King aught that may thee expose to charge,' " the ghost quoted, " 'conceal not any of thy sins however hateful its evil to tell . . . The sin a man commits in secret, much is the debt his son incurs . . . ' "

I shivered.

"And I was not being such a good father to you, either, Muirteach, neither to you nor my other bairns. I am sorry about that," he added, holding up a small, round, crystal stone. It gleamed in that ghastly candlelight.

"I have brought you a gift, by way of making it up to you. It is a charm, for protection, it is. But you must find my killer."

Even in my dream I grew irritated, with the poetry and the gift, which came too late.

"Fine I am knowing that," I replied to the phantom, "even His Lordship is telling me I must find your killer, Father. They are not wanting your death to go unavenged, nor the murder-price to go unpaid."

"No, no, Muirteach. It is not the compensation I am worrying about. Such things as that are not mattering here, not at all. You must find the killer before—"

The ghostly wind howled louder at this, and some of the candles surrounding my father flickered out.

"Before what, Father?"

"Before . . ." My father faded before my eyes. He receded from me, pulled back along some dark corridor. His voice grew fainter, but it seemed I heard him say, "Before Sheena—"

The last candle went out and the vision vanished.

I sat up in bed, awake, my heart pounding and my throat dry. There was nothing there in my house, just the faint glow of the smoldering peats from the hearth fire. Somerled snored unconcerned; whoever my ghostly visitor had been it had not disturbed my dog. I felt sure it had truly been my father's shade that had visited me in my dream, for my father had been a great one for poetry, and the songs of Muireadhach Albannach had ever been favorites of his.

I rose, went to my door, raised the door-flap and peered

outside. Darkness enfolded the world. All was still, and, except for the hammering in my chest and the rapid sound of my own breathing, quiet reigned.

I must have been riding the night mare, I told myself, brought on by too many spirits. I lay down and tried to force my breath to a slower pattern, and turned on my side to try and sleep, when I felt something under my fingers. I sat up again and looked at what I had found by the dim light of the hearth.

A small, smooth stone it was, of some quartz or crystal, round like a bird's egg and clear as ice. And then I began to sweat cold, for it was the gift my father had said he would leave for me. But it seemed to sit warmly within my fingers, and, after some time, I lay down again and fell asleep, still holding the stone in my hand, and I had no more ghastly dreams.

CHAPTER 7

Aorig had left a bowl of stew for me the night before, when I had not come to eat with them, and I awoke later to the morning light, my head pounding and the sound of a banging and thumping filling my ears. Somerled had knocked the dish from the stool, and was nosing it around on the floor as he licked up the last vestiges of my supper. I looked in my hands and the crystal stone was still there. I had not dreamed it.

I threw a half-burned peat at Somerled and he fled outside, letting the sound of voices in to my house. I fingered the stone thoughtfully, unsure what to do with it, and finally placed it in the leather pouch I wore.

I straightened my *léine*, splashed some water on my face, and wandered outside. There stood Gillespic and the Beaton. Seamus lurked hopefully on the sidelines, and Aorig and Mariota talked while Aorig sat spinning in front of her cottage. The sun was well up in the sky, and I knew I had slept far too late.

"Hello, Uncle."

"Eh, Muirteach. You are awake at last."

"Aye," I replied, not wanting to explain about the vision. "Where are you off to?"

"We were just coming down to see you," said my uncle.

"What were you wanting?"

"Mariota and I are just going over to Kilchattan to speak with that Tormod," Fearchar said. "I was wondering if you were wanting to come along."

"Were you finding the stew?" asked Aorig, pleasantly enough. "I sent Seamus with it."

"Aye, I found it, but so did Somerled."

"He is a good for nothing," said Aorig, not for the first time. I noticed the Beaton looking curiously at me.

"You are looking pale this morning, Muirteach. Were you sleeping well?"

I muttered something about waking in the night. The rest of the dream came back to me, including that final ghostly warning about Sheena. Had the spirit of my father been saying that Sheena had murdered him?

Well, it seemed I should at least go and visit her one more time. Sure enough I was that my seeing had been telling me something about Sheena. Perhaps when I arrived at her house I would know what it was.

I made some excuse or another, to the Beaton and my uncle, and set out on my way. Seamus accompanied me, along with Somerled. The day was sunny, and the breeze blew the scent of the sweet wildflowers past my nose. That put me in mind of Mariota, and for some reason my mood darkened as I walked along towards Sheena's house. I found myself wishing I had accompanied them to Kilchattan. My dream was no doubt just a fey fancy.

Seamus chattered as we walked. I am afraid I paid little mind to what he was saying; something about the harper that was here from Islay, and what a fine musician he was, but I preferred to mull over the Beaton's daughter, wondering why it was I could not get her out of my mind.

So what with one thing and another it was soon enough that we reached Sheena's holding. Smoke curled out through the smoke-hole in the thatch, but all seemed quiet. I called but no one answered immediately. Sheena, it seemed, was not at home.

I called again, and heard an answering sound, a faint crying

91

from the inside of the house, then another voice quieting the baby.

"Maire," I called, for I had recognized my half sister's voice, "Maire, come out. It is only Muirteach. Where is your mother? I would speak with her."

After another moment or so Maire emerged from the house, her arms full with the baby, who was quiet for the now, gumming what looked like a bit of a bannock.

"Mother is not here. She said we were to wait here for her. It was going to pick rush flowers she was, for dyeing the wool."

"And when was she leaving?" I asked.

"Oh, it was a long time ago, it was. The sun was just over the mountains. I hope she comes home soon, indeed, for himself is hungry and starting to fuss."

"And Sean?"

"He's away. Fishing."

The baby started to wail fretfully. Maire looked disgusted. "A silly thing he is," she said, as she put him down, sounding far older than her years. "He has wet himself again." Her nose wrinkled at the smell. "And something else as well, I'm thinking."

"Well, Maire, I am needing to spcak with your mother. I shall go looking for her, and send her home when I am finding her. Where did she go to look for her rush flowers?"

My half sister shrugged a bony shoulder. "I am thinking she went that way, towards Dun Cholla," she said, waving a hand towards the northwest, behind the cottage. "But I am not knowing for certain."

"Well, we will be looking for her, then. Take good care of your brother while you are waiting."

"She left me plenty to do," volunteered Maire, "what with the churning, and the corn to grind and all, and it is hard to be doing while I am watching him." Her face cleared. "Och, I know. I shall just be tying him to the loom. He cannot be getting into trouble then." She hefted her brother back up into her arms, turned, and went back inside.

Seamus and I left the holding with the sound of the baby's wailing wafting past us. We turned and headed northwest towards Dun Cholla, which was more or less the direction that Maire had pointed us to. I had no idea whether rush flowers grew there or not, but the turf was springy under our feet and the walking fine. We saw no signs of Sheena for a long while, although in the muddy track we saw some footprints, which made me think we were heading the right way.

We soon reached the ruins of Dun Cholla. No one had lived here for as long as I could remember, although there were stories that the Norsemen had used it in the past. Now it was sometimes used for cattle, but mostly it was abandoned. We saw no signs or anyone as we approached the ruins, the low stone walls toppled over like some giant's discarded playthings among the heather and the gorse.

"She is not here, Muirteach," said Seamus.

The sun suddenly went behind a cloud and Somerled started to whine. I felt a chill of a sudden, and shuddered.

"Let us just be looking behind the walls here," I replied. "Perhaps herself is inside, resting a bit."

We entered the ruins of the fort. The walls had tumbled to about chest height, but we had to duck through the narrow doorway. The lintel had remained in place, but the way in was so short that even the child Maire would have had to bend over to enter. I wondered who had built this place. The *sithichean* probably. It had a dank and dangerous feel to it, overgrown inside with bracken and gorse.

"She's no here, Muirteach," said Seamus, after a cursory look around. "Let's be going."

"Wait a wee while, Seamus. I think I see something. Perhaps

someone was leaving his good cloak up here."

Behind some bracken was a tumbled heap of clothing, at least that was what I thought it to be at first. As I drew closer however I saw that it was not just someone's old cloak. It was Sheena, and she looked to be dead.

CHAPTER 8

She lay on her back, her *brat* spread out on the ground beneath her. Her face showed pale against the dark green of the bracken and the cold gray of the stones. Her linen shift was rucked up around her legs, and that same thin cord mark wound around her neck, as I had seen on my father. It seemed she had been throttled, and perhaps violated, as well.

Seamus came up beside me, saw the body, then turned away. I heard the sounds of him retching in the bracken nearby. Somerled tried to nose at the body. I hurriedly pulled him away, and set him outside, then I just stared for some moments, attempting to come to terms with what I saw. One thought flashed stupidly through my brain, repeating incessantly like an endless knot design. Sheena could not have murdered my father since she, herself, was dead now. Whoever had killed my father had murdered her as well.

"Muirteach," said Seamus.

I turned to look at him. He looked pale under his freckles, almost as pale as Sheena herself.

"What shall we do?" he asked, the same question I myself had been asking.

"We should go and get the MacPhee, and the Beaton as well," I answered. "Or one of us should," I amended. "Seamus, you go, take Somerled back with you, and also be getting Mariota, or your mother. Someone will need to see to the bairns. But I'm thinking the Beaton will want to see her, before we move

95

the body. I will stay here, to watch, to make sure no dogs or whatever disturb her. And do not go by her cottage yet."

I dreaded having to tell my half sister and brothers that their mother was dead.

"Aye." Seamus looked relieved as he set off with Somerled. It was not long before he vanished from my sight and I was left alone with the dead.

It was cold and I wrapped my cloak around me, and shuddered, remembering the last words the vision of my father had said. "Before Sheena . . ." Before Sheena was murdered. I understood clearly now the meaning of his words, now, when it was too late.

Well, Father, I thought bitterly to myself, you now have yet another reason to be disappointed in your son, even from beyond the grave. For I have failed you yet again.

I knew I should be looking closely at the body but I could not bring myself to do it. Instead, I paced over the ground inside the fort, looking for anything that might prove a clue.

In the path that led to the dun, in the mud and the cow dung, I found one. A few footprints, one a woman's by the look of it, bare footed. That would be Sheena. And another print, a man's brogue, smaller in size than my own foot. The tracks entered the dun as though the two people had been walking together, at a leisurely pace. So perhaps Sheena had known her killer. It did not seem that she had fled from him at any rate.

There was a depression in the growing bracken, the path the two had taken as they wandered inside the dun, that led eventually to the corner where the body of Sheena lay. Coward that I was I avoided that area, looking instead in all the other corners of the dun for whatever I could find. There was Sheena's basket, with a bit of rush flowers in it, a partially eaten bannock, and a stoppered pottery flask. I opened it and sniffed. *Uisgebeatha*, praise be to God and all the saints.

I started to raise it to my lips, wanting some spirit in this doleful place, but stopped suddenly. With so much murder about, what if it was poisoned? I replaced the stopper and put the flask back in the basket, feeling the malice of the place even more as I resumed my search.

Circling, I finally could no longer avoid the corner where Sheena's body lay. I gathered my courage and faced her, but I could not bring myself to touch her. I would leave that to the physician. Instead I looked. There were no bruises on her throat, just the mark of that thin string around her neck. The same as the one that had wound around my father's neck. A bowstring, to be sure.

The depression in the bracken was larger in size than just her body. The green of the fern was matted next to her, as though two people had lain there together. I imagined it all, the two of them, coming into the isolated dun together, she clinging to him as they walked together, then sharing the flask, the love play, the lovemaking on the soft green fern.

And then he had strangled her, after, as she had lain next to him, with her back cuddled up against his, and her face turned away from him. That way he had not seen her eyes bulging from the sockets, her face as it reddened, then blackened, her hands as they tried, in vain, to loosen the choking cord against her.

I shivered and glanced up at the sun, halfway across the sky and starting its afternoon's descent. It would take Seamus a long while to get to Scalasaig and back again, but surely he should be returning the now.

Unwilling to stay alone with Sheena's corpse in that cold dun, I walked outside, and sat down against the wall, hoping the sun would warm me. On impulse I fished the round stone out of my pouch and stared idly into the quartz depths of it while I thought.

Who had her lover been? For certain it had not been my

father, dead and moldering in his winding sheet at the Priory. I had never heard of Sheena having another lover, but perhaps there was some talk of it among the women I did not know of. Seamus's mother might know something of the matter.

And why had he killed her, then? From their footsteps it seemed they were familiar enough with one another.

Perhaps that is why my father struck her. He learned somehow of the other lover, and then, in anger, hit her. And perhaps then the other man had lain in wait for my father in his turn, and killed him as he tried to cross the Strand.

Sheena must have known he had murdered my father, and thus he had killed her here, to keep her from speaking of it, after pleasuring himself one last time. Irreligious though I was, I crossed myself, and prayed that the Beaton would come quickly, but he did not.

At length I could stand it no longer, and despite the rays of the sun I began to shiver and shake some. I stuffed the stone back in my pouch and continued my vigil.

It seemed an eternity of days, although the sun had scarcely moved westward, before I finally heard voices and footsteps. Seamus led the way, followed by the Beaton and my uncle. But before them, crying out like the hounds of Hell themselves, were Angus and Alasdair. They were already far gone with drink, I realized, a second before they reached me. Angus grabbed me first, his hands around my throat, as he questioned me, his voice thick with drink and tears.

"And were you killing her, yourself, you coward that you are, but no, no for she cannot be dead. She is just sleeping there, in the dun, is she not?"

I knew not how to answer, nor could I, with his hands choking me so, and it was a relief when my uncle reached me and wrested Angus's hands from my throat. I wheezed and gasped for breath, and shook my head, still unable to answer, while he continued his rant.

"Hold them back now, Gillespic," ordered the Beaton, "while I go inside and see what's amiss here." He gestured me to come with him, and I was glad to, away from the raging bulls that were Sheena's grieving brothers.

"Where did you find them?" I asked the Beaton when we were safe inside the dun and away from their ears. "Could they have done it?"

"They were far gone with the drink at Donald Dubh's," replied the Beaton, "and had been, all morning. There are many who will vouch for them."

"So they did not do this," I said.

The Beaton scowled at me. "Muirteach," he said patiently, in the way of someone explaining things to a child, "are you truly thinking they would do this to their own sister?" And I had to confess that I had not really thought they had done so. But then who had?

"Time enough to be dealing with that, later on," he answered, "but first let us look at her, poor thing."

The Beaton's examination of the body was a hurried one; the sounds of Angus and Alasdair's wailing outside made it so. I was glad to see him gently straighten her clothing a bit, pulling her shift down over her legs and covering her body with her *brat,* thus giving her a more modest appearance, before Gillespic and Seamus could prevent her brothers from bursting in on us.

"Och, my white love, *mo chridhe,* my heart, you have gone from us, and whatever will your bairns be doing the now, without their mother and whatever shall we be doing without you as well?" Alasdair moaned. I was surprised to see him grieve so, which proved how little I knew the man at that time.

Angus, more stolid in his grief, just sat on the ground near his sister's body, ramming his dirk into the ground nearby again, and again, and again. His face white, his upper teeth bit down hard upon his lower lip, so hard, indeed, that the blood trickled from it, while the little pile of disturbed black earth grew around the blade of his knife, dark like blood against the green bracken.

The Beaton looked grim, and reached in the satchel he carried for a small glass vial, which he handed towards my uncle. "Here, mix some of this with *uisgebeatha*. It is poppy juice, from the Levant. It will calm them, a bit, for the while."

Gillespic nodded, and took the vial, pouring a good portion of it into his own flask of whiskey, then he handed Alasdair the flask, and Alasdair stopped his rant long enough to drink a long swig. My uncle then looked at Angus, holding the flask towards him, but the man stared right through him, still driving his knife into the ground.

My uncle shrugged his shoulders somewhat and seemed a bit at a loss, which was unusual for him. I could not remember ever seeing him in such a way before. But he collected himself, and said, as Alasdair finished his drink and before he could begin keening again, "Now, Alasdair you must be gathering yourself together the now, man. We cannot be leaving her here, but must be laying her out proper, like."

"Aye," said Alasdair, stopping his mourning a moment to consider. "We shall lay her out with candles, and masses, beeswax candles if we can get them. In the church it shall be. Angus, you, stop playing with your knife. We must be carrying our sister home. We cannot be leaving her here, in this place. Put your dirk away, the now, and be a man about it."

I think my uncle was relieved when Angus slowly sheathed his dirk, and lumbered to his feet. I know I was.

We made a makeshift stretcher from a *brat* and two branches of rowan growing nearby, and carried my stepmother—for such in a sense she was, although she was but a few years older than myself—back to her cottage. Seamus told me that Mariota had taken the bairns away with Aorig, to her house. I was glad I did not have to look in the face of my half sister and brothers as I carried the dead body of their mother over the threshold of the cottage.

But perhaps the children knew something of this—at least who their mother had been going to meet that morning when she had gone out to pick her rush flowers. Or perhaps the man had visited the cottage before that. So it was that, after we had placed the corpse on the mound of bracken that had served as Sheena's mattress, I went, all unwillingly, in search of my brothers and sister, while the Beaton remained with Angus and Alasdair, to wait for the women from Scalasaig who would come to lay out the body.

I found them at Aorig's, as Seamus had told me I would. Maire, her little face pinched, was looking after the baby while her brother ran wildly around the cottage, scaring Aorig's chickens and terrorizing the hen. Aorig seemed but a little flustered.

"Och, I had forgotten what banshees the little ones can be," she said easily. "Mind you, do not be scaring my hen so that she will not be laying," she called to my half brother. "Maire, you can put the bairn down, now. He will be safe enough, sleeping here."

Maire did not answer, but sat rocking her baby brother back and forth in front of the hearth.

"Do they know?" I asked Aorig in an undertone.

"Eh, we have told them nothing, the poor lambs, but Maire is knowing that something is amiss."

"Well, who is going to be telling them?" I asked peevishly. I knew I did not want to be the one to do it. "And where is Mariota?"

Aorig gave me a shrewd glance. "Mariota left the bairns here with me. She said she had something to see to. She did not tell

101

me what it was."

"And as to who will be telling the poor bairns," she continued, "that I do not know." Her face looked worried underneath her white kerch. "Mayhap Angus and Alasdair? Or Gillespic? He is their uncle also." She looked at me a little accusingly. "You are their half brother, after all, Muirteach. Mayhap you should tell them. You are here, after all."

"I do not think so," I said quickly. "But I would like to be speaking with Maire."

Aorig shrugged, and motioned me towards the hearth. I sat down on the three-legged stool next to my half sister. "Maire," I said. "Maire, it is just Muirteach. Will you speak with me?"

"Where is Mother?"

I could not lie to her, but I could not tell her what had happened. "Your mother has had an accident, white love," I finally managed to say.

I was somewhat relieved when Maire did not ask any more, but the dejected slump of her head as she bent over her baby brother, crooning some nonsense song to him, led me to think I would not be needing to tell her the rest.

"Maire," I finally asked, "did your mother speak of meeting with anyone today, this morning, when she left to get her rush flowers? Or did anyone visit in the last few days, anyone unusual at all?"

Maire bit her lip. "No, she was going to get the plants, that was all." I watched her little teeth gnaw on her thin lower lip a little. "For dyeing the wool," she added, as if she thought a man like myself would not know what it was for. "I wish she would come home," she suddenly said. "My brother is aye fretful, now. Herself"—she pointed her chin in Aorig's direction—"was giving him some cow's milk to drink but it will be giving him the colic."

"And no one visited?" I persisted, not wanting to be the one to tell her that her mother would not be coming home.

"No one," she said, her little jaw snapping shut tight.

I sighed and rose up from the stool, starting to leave.

"What happened to your leg?" my half sister suddenly asked.

I flushed like a maid. I hate to be asked about my leg, and I hated it even more in those days. "I had a fever," I said shortly, "when I was about the age of your brother outside. It stopped growing, and when it did grow, it grew twisted. That was the way of it."

She gave me a searching look, then went back to crooning her lullaby without saying anything more. I left the cottage, feeling oddly nonplussed.

Outside I found that Mariota had returned. "And where were you?" I asked, sounding perhaps surlier than I truly felt. But somehow I had wanted her here, taking care of my brothers and sisters, so that I would not be worried by it.

"Away to your aunt's to get a poppet for the child and some remedy for the colic for your baby brother," she replied, the silver of her voice as even as the still waters of Loch Fada on a calm day. "Maire is not a grown woman. She should have a poppet, or something. Now that one," she said, indicating my other brother, who had not stopped his efforts at upsetting Aorig's homestead, "knows how to play far too well."

I shrugged in agreement, for by now my younger brother had gotten Aorig's spindle and was charging at the dun cow with it, pretending it was a spear and the cow a stag. It took some time for Aorig to reclaim her spindle, swat my half brother on his bum, and sit down again at her work. After all was calm again, I gestured to Mariota.

"Walk with me."

"Oh?"

"I need to speak with you, where those ones cannot be hearing."

She smiled, unruffled by my bad humor, and we set out to walk up the path towards Brigit's well.

"So Angus and Alasdair could not have done this," I said.

"And it is clear that Sheena did not kill your father," Mariota added, when I had told her about the cord mark on Sheena's neck, "for whoever killed him, killed her. Yet not so violently. Or," she continued, her white brow furrowed a little in thought, "it could well have been someone who knew how your father was killed, and tried to imitate that."

"Perhaps."

"What of the canons?"

I supposed one of the canons could have killed Sheena. But would he have lain with her first? I thought of my father and shrugged. Why not? Sheena had not scrupled to sleep with those in Holy Orders, as my three half brothers and sisters proved.

I wondered if Brother Donal had found anything else at the Priory. Sure it did not seem that Columbanus would murder his sister, but what of Gillecristus? If he had murdered my father, in hopes of becoming the next Prior, and somehow Sheena had known of it, might he have killed her to keep his secret?

And Columbanus did not know yet of his sister's death. Perhaps I should go tell him of it.

Mariota agreed that sounded a fine idea.

We neared the well, with its fine view towards the north. You could see almost to the golden sands of Kiloran, and Dun Nan Nighean, where the chief's wives were sent to give birth. I pointed out these sites to Mariota, by way of hoping to impress her a bit.

"A fine thing, that," she said, "to have your wife climb up there to give birth, up in that dun."

"It is not so bad," I pointed out, "at least my aunt has done well by it. All her bairns have been healthy, at least." I thought of my leg, suddenly, and flushed.

We stopped at the spring. There were some rags tied to the branches of the nearby gorse bush, gifts to the saint, and in the pool formed by the spring was the glint of silver and copper coins thrown there by the devout.

Mariota knelt, and I listened to her sweet voice repeat the old blessing of Brigit, while I tried to pray myself.

Brigit of the mantles,
Brigit of the peat-heap,
Brigit of the shining hair,
Brigit of the augury,
Nor fire shall burn me.
Nor sun shall burn me
Nor moon shall blanch me
Nor water shall drown me
Nor flood shall drown me
Nor brine shall drown me
Nor seed of fairy host shall lift me
Nor seed of airy host shall lift me
Nor earthly being destroy me.

Mariota took a ribbon from her bag and tied it on one of the branches of the shrub growing near the well. Then she plunged her hands into the water welling from the crevice in the rocks, and drank deeply.

She looked so lovely kneeling there, the sweet, sweet form of her, with her long hair in plaits down her back, hanging heavily like chains of white gold. I made my own wish, hopeless as it seemed at the time, and reached into my pouch for something to offer the saint. I touched the round stone within and fancied my fingers tingled as they felt it.

I found a bit of copper to offer the saint and flung it into the pool. It sank to the bottom of the peat-stained water, disappearing into a crevice in the rocks. Then I took my own draught from the blessed spring; the water cooled my parched throat after the steep climb.

"And what did you ask Brigit for?" Mariota said to me, as we turned back towards Scalasaig. But I did not tell her.

CHAPTER 9

I took my uncle's small boat and returned to the Priory, but the afternoon was far gone before I arrived there. The sun that had shone so weakly earlier in the day had vanished, and fog had rolled in, making the Priory look almost like just another pile of wet rocks heaped up on the coast. The mist muffled most of the noises of the masons, finishing their day's work on the north range. There had always been some few culdees on Oronsay, but it was only since the days of His Lordship that the Augustinian Priory had been built.

Perhaps the Lord of the Isles intended his gifts to the Priory to pave his way into heaven, I thought sourly to myself, but all the noise of the masons seemed to place Oronsay squarely in the mundane world. In the evening, however, the masons returned to their cottages nearby, and the Priory became more peaceful.

Word had evidently not reached them of Sheena's death. The tide had been in, and the monastery cut off from the main island except by boat, and word was that no boats had docked there that day.

The canons were just leaving the refectory after their evening meal and I sought out Brother Donal, after first speaking briefly with Gillecristus. I did not tell him of Sheena's death, but merely said I needed to ask some of the brothers a few more questions.

"Now?" questioned Gillecristus. "It will soon be time for Vespers."

"Yes," I said shortly.

Gillecristus shrugged, his face sour, and left me to find Brother Donal. We strolled down towards the cove, where there was little chance of being overheard, while the sun, finding its way through the clouds, broke through the dispersing fog and began to descend in the western sky.

"So have you discovered anything?" I asked Donal bluntly.

"Och, Muirteach," he said, wrapping his habit a little more tightly around him as the wind blew against his thin body. "Well, they are saying this; that Gillecristus will be our new Prior."

"So he could have had a reason to kill my father."

Donal shrugged, his face glowing in the sunset.

I told him about what had happened to Sheena, and my suspicions. "So suppose Gillecristus murdered Sheena because she knew what he had done. Perhaps she walked down after my father to the Strand that night, and saw Gillecristus kill him, and then she had to die."

"But then why would he have lain with her? Or she with him?" said Donal, and I had to admit that that did not fit. Gillecristus was a dried-up stick, not a lusty man as my father had been. I simply could not picture him following Sheena to Dun Cholla and her submitting to him, for there had been no signs of violence except that last done there.

"Where was Gillecristus this morning?" I asked.

"I did not see him this morning, Muirteach," Donal replied, looking troubled. "He had left word he was fasting and doing penance in his chamber this morning. He does so frequently, and I thought little of it at the time."

"And Columbanus?"

"In his bake-house I suppose. Although young Blaise is ill in the infirmary, and he helps with the baking most times. So it may be that Columbanus was there alone, with none to vouch for him, either."

"It is unlikely to be Columbanus, though," I added. "He would not lie with his sister."

"Pray to God he would not," returned Donal. "Such a sin as that would be. But men have done worse, even than that, in this world."

I agreed that they had.

The rays of the sinking sun glimmered crimson on the waves and we turned our steps back to the Priory. I now had the unpleasant task of telling Columbanus about his sister. I wondered that Angus and Alasdair had not done so, but realized they were probably too far gone with drink to be going anywhere or telling anyone anything by now.

Donal came with me, and I was glad of that. We found Columbanus in his bake-house, stirring down some proofing yeast in a large pottery bowl. His face reddened with anger when he saw me.

"And what brings you back here," he said. "Be away from here, you will sour my yeast."

"No, now," Donal put in. "Calm yourself, Columbanus. Muirteach is bringing some sad news indeed from the main island."

"It is your sister, Columbanus. Sheena. She is dead." I spoke abruptly for I did not know how else to tell him.

I had feared Columbanus would be as demonstrative in his grief as his brothers had been. But instead he stood dumbly, like a cow, and stared at me.

"Dead?"

"Aye. You were not knowing of it?"

"How did she die?"

"She was murdered, Columbanus. Like my father. At Dun Cholla."

He lunged at me, and I was glad there were no weapons in the bake-house.

"But who would murder Sheena?" he asked, after Brother Donal and I had succeeded in quieting him. He had proved not so different from his brothers after all. "What had she ever done to anyone?"

"I do not know," I answered carefully. "But could it not be the same person who killed my father? Perhaps she saw something of the first murder, perhaps she had gone down to the Strand after him for something, and then saw it, and so the murderer had to kill her."

"Your father was a bastard, Muirteach, as you yourself are. And now, in his death, he has killed my sister."

I bit my lip so hard that I tasted blood, as I tried to control myself from lunging at Columbanus in my turn.

"It is the shock talking, Muirteach," said Donal soothingly to me. "Sure, you are not meaning this, Columbanus, not about our own dead Prior, may God grant him eternal rest."

"And am I not meaning it?" roared Columbanus. "The black heart of him. He will rot in Hell for what he has done. All those years he took what he wanted from our family, leaving only wreckage in his wake. And now, you are telling me he has killed my sister—"

"Whist, no, now, Columbanus," said Donal. "He was not killing your sister, the man is already dead, and Prior or no, the good Lord himself is deciding where he will rest, in Heaven or in Hell. But he did not kill your sister. Someone else must answer for that crime."

"But if she died because of what she had seen—"

"You still cannot be holding the Prior responsible for that. You must have faith, faith in the mercy and justice of Our Lord."

"And what justice was there for her?" Columbanus asked challengingly, but neither Donal nor myself could answer that question for him.

Columbanus went back with me, to see to his sister. As I rowed back to Colonsay through the darkness, for the sun had finally set, I said, in a manner of preparing him, as it were, "Sheena was strangled, Columbanus. With a cord. It could have been a bowstring. Are you knowing anyone who would have such a cord? Do your brothers?"

I asked this because I wondered if he knew anything more. The cord Sheena was strangled with could have been any string, I supposed, but it would have had to be strong to do that hellish work, for it had cut horribly into her flesh. I could not drive the image from my mind. It leapt and tumbled in my brain, mixed with images of my father's corpse, with every stroke of the oars.

Columbanus snorted in disgust. "Who on the islands does not have a bow, Muirteach? What kind of *amadan* asks that question? When last I heard, both Angus and Alasdair had fine bows, but so did all the other men on Colonsay."

He was right. Every man on the islands had a bow, for hunting the red deer, and even coneys for the stew pot. And so, as I beached the boat and we climbed the path leading to Sheena's cottage by moonlight, I still had no clue as to who had killed her.

The house was crowded although the hour was now late. The women had finished the laying out and now the wake was on in earnest, the women keening and the men drinking, for the most part. The body lay on a trestle table surrounded by candles, while pitch torches burned, set in holders on the stone walls. The flames leapt and danced in the glowering darkness of the hut, casting glinting lights on the silver coins that covered Sheena's eyes and flickering shadows of the mourners, like the hosts of the *sìthichean*, against the walls of the house.

I watched as Columbanus found and embraced his brothers, and the three, looking oddly alike despite the tonsure and robes of Columbanus, stood together looking at the corpse of their sister. Little Maire was there too, along with my older half brother, and I wondered who it was that had finally told them what I had been too cowardly to tell them—that their mother was dead. The women sang their keening song over the corpse:

You are going home this night to your home of winter,
To your home of autumn, of spring, of summer,
You are going home this night to your lasting home,
To your unending rest, to your lasting bed.

Maire's eyes were red as she listened—she would have been crying, of course—but her face was white as the linen shroud that wrapped her mother. Her brother stood by her side, wide-eyed, uncharacteristically solemn and quiet, with snot and tears mixed together running down his cheek. I did not see the baby, or Aorig, and I guessed that she had kept him at her house.

But Mariota was there, along with her father, and she smiled at me a little when she saw me through the crush of people. I was surprised when she made her way to my side. She plucked at my sleeve and drew me towards the door of the cottage, away from the crush by the bier.

"I need to speak with you," she said urgently. We went outside, and sat on a large rock overlooking the sound. The sounds of mourning and talk from inside Sheena's cottage wafted out to us, mingled with the sound of the waves on the shoreline below, while the full moon had risen and its light glinted silver on the rocks and the water.

"And so?" she asked, expectantly.

"What?"

She frowned a little, but it looked more like a half-smile. "What were you finding out when you went to see Donal?"

"It was for that you needed to speak with me?"

"Aye."

I did not then understand women. Nor, I can say, do I even understand them the now. But I answered her question.

"Gillecristus looks in a fair way to be becoming the next Prior. And Columbanus knew nothing of his sister's death before I arrived."

"Well, what of Gillecristus?"

"He was not seen this morning. He told the other canons he was alone in his chamber, fasting, and doing penance. So it could have been him, I suppose. He, or Columbanus, could have slipped away, taken the coracle across the Strand, met her, killed her, and returned with none the wiser. But did Sheena know Gillecristus? Sheena knew her killer, she was friendly with him."

"And she could not have been friendly, as you call it, with Gillecristus?"

I scowled. "I cannot think so, Mariota," I answered with some exasperation, as if I was speaking to a child. "He is a dried-up old stick of a man, and neither Donal nor myself think that he would have abused Sheena before he killed her. Gillecristus continually spoke against her. He did not think it seemly for the Prior to have a handfasted wife. He felt it took him too much away from his duties. He felt it his mission, I believe, to point this out often to my father. Which he did do, repeatedly."

Mariota just smiled, and I felt compelled to add something more to my speech. "Gillecristus is forever speaking about the snares and wiles that women use to entrap men and lure them into sin. For you do know, do you not, that Eve was the cause of Man's fall from Paradise."

Mariota continued to smile, more broadly now, and I got the distinct feeling she was trying to keep from laughing. For myself, I could not believe how much I myself had sounded like Gillecristus himself as I had spoken.

"And you, do you believe that, Muirteach?" she asked.

"Well, it is the teaching of the Church." I felt myself flushing and felt my tongue all tied in knots. Why was she asking such questions? And why had I even brought up the topic, at all, at all? "But I left the order," I continued somewhat lamely. "I found I would not make a monk."

CHAPTER 10

"And why was that?"

I did not answer and then I thought I noticed that Mariota herself was blushing, although it was difficult to tell in the moonlight. But whether she was or no, it did not stop her from continuing to speak.

"Well, whatever, perhaps even such a pious man as Gillecristus might find himself ensnared by a woman's wiles. It might not be impossible, no matter how unlikely." Her eyebrows arched as she looked at me. "You do not think so?"

I stuttered a moment, red-faced like a lad, and then grudgingly admitted it was possible.

"Well, that is settled, then," she said a moment later, her tone strangely brisk. "But that still is not to say that it was Gillecristus was the killer."

"But you were just arguing that it was," I said, bemused.

"No, Muirteach, I was speaking of something else entirely. But perhaps I had no business to have been speaking of it." She paused.

We sat in silence for a moment listening to the waves, and the clamor from the house. People were drinking more now, and I could hear the voices of Angus and Alasdair and Columbanus as they mourned their sister.

"Muirteach," Mariota asked abruptly, "when you were finding Sheena, was she wearing a fine brooch on her plaid?"

"No," I answered. I thought I remembered the pin Mariota

was thinking of. "That same fine silver pin she was wearing to the funeral? I do not think she would be wearing it to pick rush flowers."

"No," replied Mariota, "but she might indeed wear it if she was going to meet her lover. We did not find it, Muirteach, when we laid out her body. It is not here at her house. I looked for it."

I was puzzled. "What of that? She could well have lost it."

Mariota looked at me, and even in the dim light I could read her expression. "She wore it just the day before, at the funeral. A woman does not lose a pin like that, Muirteach, nor does she misplace it. And especially not a woman like Sheena, who has so little. I think she wore it to meet her murderer and he took it from her body after he had killed her. Find the pin and we find the murderer. I am thinking that brooch will tell us who the murderer is."

"Aye," I responded sourly, "and it will tell us that whoever killed her is a thief and stole her fine brooch out of greed."

"There is another thing, Muirteach. Sheena was breeding, she was going to have a child."

"How are you knowing that?" I asked. "And why were you not telling me earlier?"

"Muirteach, I was with the women when we were doing the laying out. There were signs, in her breasts and her belly. I am thinking she was three or four months gone, not so much as you might be noticing, but we could tell."

"And so? Are you thinking that is why she was murdered? It makes no sense."

"No, and she was not so large that people would know."

"Unless she did have another lover, and he killed her, the child would have been my father's."

"And so it would have been your own sister or brother. It is a sad thing, indeed."

Again we said nothing for awhile, each of us keeping our thoughts to ourselves.

"I will be returning to Islay soon," Mariota said abruptly.

"Oh?"

"Yes, my father means to return tomorrow, and I will go with him then. Perhaps I can see if any of the MacDonalds from the Rhinns were missing when your father died, and again this morning. And there are other things I must be seeing to there, as well."

I will own I felt strangely disappointed when she said she must leave. Although why it would be mattering to me, I could not at the time imagine. A woman with a sharp tongue, Mariota was—for all that she had a sweet smile, and cheeks like berries, and the long golden hair of her—but she had a sharp tongue, for all of that, and I always felt myself to be getting in the way of it. The way she smiled at me, I felt she laughed at me somehow, as if I amused her in secret.

So I did not ask what other business she had in Islay, only muttered something in reply. If I had asked, it might have saved me some grief. Or perhaps, even had I known, it would have made no difference whatever in the way things worked themselves out. But that bit of the tale comes later.

A figure left the house and approached us in the moonlight. I stiffened, fearing that Angus had decided to come out and stick his dirk in my back, but as the man drew closer I saw it was Fearchar. Then I wondered what he would think, to see me sitting here in the moonlight with his daughter, for all that there had been nothing whatever to it. For, I told myself sternly, she would never have a cripple, and I was not wanting her either. I would never be getting any rest from that tongue of hers, and that laughter that she had.

"Och, Father," said Mariota as he approached, "I was just telling Muirteach that I would be returning to Islay with you when you go tomorrow."

"Aye?"

"Yes." She sounded very decided. "I have business to see to, as you well know, Father. And I was promising Muirteach that we would look into the MacDonalds of the Rhinns, those that were related to his mother, on that side, and be making sure that none of them were leaving oddly like, last week and last night, to be killing the Prior and poor Sheena. Now what were you saying their names were, Muirteach? And who would be most likely to be wanting revenge for your mother's sake?"

I told her their names, although it had been a long while since I had seen my Islay relatives, and as to who would be most likely to revenge himself on my father I could not guess. Colonsay was my home now, and had been since I had been a child of five, when I had gone to live with Uncle Gillespic after my mother's death.

"So that is settled then. I will go with you, Father, tomorrow."

The Beaton agreed. "Fine I know that once Mariota gets an idea into her head, Muirteach, there is no talking her out of it. She was like that with learning the medicine from me, as a girl. She would not be taking 'no' as an answer, but must be going with me wherever I went. And so many questions she had, even then."

I saw him smile with fondness at his daughter in the moonlight. "And so she will be talking to your relatives, Muirteach, and woe to them if they were not where they should have been on these days."

"When will you be leaving?" I asked, not smiling back.

"We will leave after Sheena's funeral Mass tomorrow."

So that was that, then, and there seemed little else to say. After a time I left the Beaton and his daughter sitting in the moonlight, went back inside to the wake, and got myself very drunk on Angus and Alasdair's whiskey.

Sheena's funeral, the next morning, was a sad affair. The priest
was hung over, as was I. He also had been at the wake the night
before. Rain fell steadily, and the lowering sky blocked the view
of anything more than a few hundred yards distant. The sound I
remember the most is the sobbing of Maire and her brother
when the first clods of earth fell upon their mother's shrouded
body in the grave.

Mariota and her father took their leave soon after, and I
retreated to Donald Dubh's. I spent the rest of the long gray
afternoon there, listening to the harper from Islay, telling myself
I was listening out for any gossip or clues that might be revealed
there.

When I emerged some four hours later it was still raining.
The village of Scalasaig had become a fine morass, what with
mud churned by the passing of villagers, mixed with cow and
sheep dung. I headed for my house, unsteady on my feet as I
was, berating myself. There was something I was missing,
something I was not seeing, or I would have found my father's
murderer by now.

I thought that, if Mariota wanted to seek out clues among my
long-lost relations on Islay, she was welcome to the task. It
would keep her from pestering me.

I wandered into my house, which was cold, and tried to light
a fire on the hearth to drive some of the afternoon's chill away.
But the peats were wet, there being a hole in the thatch that I
had not attended to, and so after shivering in the dark for awhile
I left and went next door to Aorig's.

It was cozy there, no leaking thatch, and Aorig was baking
some bannocks. Seamus played with my half brothers, crawling
on all fours being ridden like a horse by Sean, which made
Maire actually smile just a wee bit and the baby coo with

laughter. They came in a fair way close to knocking over the dish of meal that Aorig had set on a stool next to the hearth where she was working, but she only smiled at me and did not stop them. It only needed Somerled to complete the picture of total chaos, but I had left him sleeping on my mattress, which I knew would smell of wet dog when I returned to lie myself down upon it later that night.

"It is a fine thing to see them laughing a bit, after the sad day they have had, poor bairns."

"And so will they be staying with you, then?" I asked.

Aorig shrugged. "I am happy enough to have them, for the while. I do not see them doing well with those great louts of bachelors, their uncles. No offense meant to you Muirteach, but it is taking a woman to know how to be raising bairns."

I had no wish to deny that, and no wish for bairns of my own, at all, so I said nothing much in reply, but listened while Aorig chattered and enjoyed the smell of the hot bannocks which soon filled the small house.

"And so you have no wish to marry, Muirteach?"

I snorted with what I supposed was a laugh, and banished the thought of Mariota's face from my mind. "And who would have me, Aorig?" I said with some bravado.

"There are those that would have you, I am thinking," said Aorig. "You are not so ill-favored as all that, with that dark hair and those gray eyes that you have."

"No, no, Aorig," I denied, "I've no wish to be married."

"There are some women," Aorig persisted, "who would like a man with a good mind, one who can read and write."

"Well, I am not knowing of any," I said shortly, my mood darkening for some reason I did not completely understand.

Just then Seamus, acting far younger than his fourteen years, crashed against the bed in the corner and little Sean fell onto the floor, bumped his forehead and began to wail. In the ensuing confusion, to my great relief, the topic was dropped.

Aorig's husband entered. He also had been at Donald Dubh's but had the wisdom to return home for dinner. He had had enough of his wife's tongue-lashings in the past, I guessed. Or perhaps it was that Aorig's cooking was too fine to pass up. And he had brought a guest with him home, as well. The harper followed him in the door, his fine harp bundled up well against the rain on his back.

"Whist, white love," said Aorig's husband crossing to the hearth where she was cooking, and giving her a somewhat well-whiskeyed kiss, "look who I am bringing back with me."

"Fine I can see you are not alone," said Aorig as she sighed and reached for more meal to make more bannocks. The children, meanwhile, stopped their playing and shyly watched the new arrivals from the corner.

"He said he would be playing for us in return for some of your fine cooking. And I was not such an *amadan* as to refuse such an offer. He is a fine harper, now Aorig, and you will be thanking me for this, do not fear."

"I am sure that I will be," said his wife, as she bent to stir the stew. "Here now, it is just ready. You can sit, and eat now. I am thinking you are needing some food in you, to sober you up. You are welcome," she said to the bard. "Sit you down, and eat your fill."

He was a fine figure of a man, the bard was, with long hair to his shoulders, a thin braid falling down one side of it. His hair and the beard on his face had a glint of bronze in the gold of it, while his nose was hooked like the beak of an eagle. I guessed he was about my own age, or perhaps just a few years older, although from the weathered look of his face he had spent more of his years out under the sky than I had, at my scriving.

"And are you liking our island?" asked Aorig, as the man ate.

"It is fine enough," the harper replied, before he raised the bowl to his lips to drink the last of the good broth in the stew. "But I soon will be traveling onward, perhaps to Mull. The Mac-Lean of Duart is kind to traveling musicians."

We all ate our fill of the good stew, and afterwards, while her husband and I both basked in the glow of a full stomach and a mind eased by the *uisgebeatha,* we all sat by the fire, the bairns gathered around Aorig's knees, and the harper played for us. Such sweet music he made with his strings. There was a wildness in his playing, just held in check, which roused all manner of longings in me, and I found tears rolling down my cheeks, tears even for my dead father, and other things which would never be.

"Such a talent you have," Aorig complimented him after the last notes died away into the glow of the peat fire, like the twinkling of the last star when the sun is lightening the sky. "And you have no settled home? You are no chief's bard?"

"I am my own man," replied the harper in a terse voice. "I belong to no one." His tone made it obvious that no more inquiries were welcome, and so I left Aorig's to return to my own mattress, and roused Somerled to move his great bulk onto the floor. As I lay there, the smell of wet dog filling my nostrils, I had no insight as to what would cause a man to lead such a life of wandering. But his music filled my dreams that night.

CHAPTER 11

The next day Aorig took Maire and Sean back to their mother's cottage, to get some belongings. I took my uncle's small boat and went back to the Priory, and Columbanus returned with me. He had stayed with his brothers the night after the funeral. His time away from the Priory did not look to have done him much good. His eyes were bloodshot and red, and he seemed to have a sore aching in his head, to judge from the way he squinted at the sunlight on the water, and the groans he uttered each time the boat leapt up in the waves.

"We heard some fine music last night," I finally said, when the sound of his retching over the side of the boat had subsided a bit. "Aorig's husband brought that harper home from Donald Dubh's. A fine hand he has for the music, that one."

Columbanus looked at me as he rinsed his mouth out with some salt water and spat it out over the rail.

"He puts me in mind of someone who once was a novice at the Priory, a long while ago. But he said nothing of it, so perhaps he is not the same man."

"Oh?" I waited while Columbanus retched over the side of the coracle and a wave washed over the side. "Be careful," I admonished. "You'll be tipping us all in the water."

Just then we reached the Priory, and Columbanus dragged himself off to his bakeshop. He would be having plenty to confess at the next chapter meeting, I thought to myself, and I felt a sudden surge of gladness that I no longer was a part of this community. But that realization solved no murders.

I asked to see Gillecristus. What with Sheena's murder, I had not spoken to him of his argument with my father, or of Tormod's accident. I felt the time had come, although the thought of it gave me a queasy feeling in my gut. I did not relish this, but sure with His Lordship breathing down my neck like MacPhee's black dog himself, I felt I had little choice in it all.

Gillecristus consented to see me in the Prior's small withdrawing room. There was a table in the room, and a large carved chair, while the walls were painted with scenes showing the Last Judgment. On one side Christ reigned over the chosen, while on the others black and blue devils poked at the damned with pitchforks and pushed them into the yawning maw of Hell, filled with fiery flames. It was not a peaceful picture and I confess I felt like one of the damned as I stood before Gillecristus.

"You may sit there," said Gillecristus, indicating a stool in front of the table. I sat down and waited a moment before I spoke.

"There are a few things I am needing to ask you," I finally said. "His Lordship is aye anxious to have this completed and to find the killer of my father."

"As are we all," said Gillecristus.

"You were hearing that Columbanus's sister was murdered?"

Gillecristus turned a shade paler. "The whore. It is better than she deserved. Aye, I had heard. That is why Columbanus was gone the past two days."

"She leaves three bairns."

"Bastards. As are you, Muirteach."

I flinched. I could not help it. I breathed in deeply before I replied, hoping my voice sounded calm.

"What reason have you to hate Sheena, so, Gillecristus?" I

asked the sub-prior. "She was not the only handfasted wife my father had."

"Aye, but she was the only one he flaunted so. She took him away from his duties. It was here he should have been, Muirteach, seeing to the Priory and the spiritual needs of this community. And it was she who tempted him to such evil, with the sinfulness of her body, like Eve's, which tempted Adam away from Paradise."

"I am thinking that the sin was not all on Sheena's side," I interjected, and watched Gillecristus's Adam's apple bob up and down in his throat as he struggled to reply.

"If it had not been for her temptation, Crispinus would not have strayed so from his duties. Nor would he have flaunted his misdeeds so. It was as though he enjoyed it—others knowing that his mistress lived just across the Strand, there, a short walk away. I would know whenever he went to her; he would not hide it."

I watched Gillecristus knot his hands together, so tightly that his bony knuckles went white, and waited for him to continue speaking.

"Indeed he seemed to enjoy taunting me with it. 'I am just going over the Strand this evening, Gillecristus,' he would tell me, and then he would give me a leer and a wink, and leave the Prior's house. I would imagine him swiving her, again and again, tupping her as an old ram does a ewe, for all the hours he was gone from here. It was a whore of Babylon, she was, and no mistake, dressed in her cloth of scarlet and gold, seducing him from his duties here."

Whenever I had seen Sheena she had been wearing rough wool, not silks of scarlet or cloth of gold, but I somehow resisted pointing this out to Gillecristus.

"I have heard you were not seen the morning Sheena was murdered, Gillecristus. Where were you?" I asked.

I watched his choler grow. "You are not accusing me!"

"Och, no, I am not, Gillecristus, but you have just made it clear you did not like the woman. Where were you on that day?"

"I was fasting, doing penance for my sins. I did not leave my room that day."

"What sins, Gillecristus?"

He did not answer me.

I guessed his whereabouts could be proven or disproven, somehow, if I questioned the other canons. Surely someone would have seen him if he had left his chamber.

"Were you knowing that Sheena was with child, Gillecristus, when she was killed?"

He blanched, swallowed, then finally spoke, his voice harsh. "Then that is what comes of her whoring with him. Four times a whore, that makes her."

I said nothing for a moment, then spoke. "I was hearing that you had quarreled with my father shortly before he died. Something about the masons, it was?"

Gillecristus did not deny it. "Aye, I did, and to my great sorrow. It was that Calum Glas. A fine enough mason before the drink gets to him, but then he becomes careless. But your father would hear nothing against him, for they are kin. And poor Tormod suffers now because of it."

"You are kin with Tormod, are you not?"

"Aye, on his mother's side. But what of that?"

I let that go. It would not do to be openly accusing the next Prior of Oronsay of murder, at least not until I knew for sure he had killed my father. But Gillecristus caught my thread of thought.

"Surely, Muirteach, you cannot be thinking that I had anything to do with your father's death." His face blanched white, then reddened, then paled again with the force of his emotions. "God forgive me, Muirteach, I loved your father. He was my soul friend. I would not kill him, not over a silly quarrel over some construction."

"But, as you say, Tormod now suffers due to my father's negligence."

"No, that is putting too strong a point to it, Muirteach. Tormod is suffering now because it is God's will he do so."

"Well, then," I asked, feeling suddenly reckless, "if you would not kill to revenge Tormod, would you kill to become the next Prior? Would you kill my father out of your own ambition? Is that the sin you did penance for?"

I thought the man would have a fit. As he sputtered his denials I felt the time had come to take my leave, and did so with alacrity.

I sought out Brother Donal, finding him in the Scriptorium. I confess I found comfort in speaking with him, as there was much in these murders that troubled me. I first told him of my conversation with Gillecristus. Donal looked doubtful.

"I know they quarreled, Muirteach, but I do not think Gillecristus has it in him to kill over that. Nor do I think he would do so to avenge a foolish, headstrong boy too hasty to check the safety of his own scaffolding, for all that the lad might be his kin."

"And what of his ambition?"

"He was close with your father, Muirteach, and had been for many years. The two of them have been here since Lord John endowed the Priory, more than twenty years ago now. They often disagreed about the best way to do things, but, no, I do not think Gillecristus would murder his soul friend over such matters. Why now?" He sighed.

Then there was the matter of Sheena's murder. Brother Donal could not see Gillecristus lying with a woman, then strangling her, but was unable to say for sure whether Gillecristus had left his chamber that morning. Although I myself, remembering the force of Gillecristus's speech, thought he might well kill a woman if he knew she was pregnant by him, or felt himself ensnared by her wiles.

Columbanus's comment in the boat nagged at me, and I asked Donal about the runaway novice.

"Och yes, I remember him well," he answered. "Your father was aye upset when the lad left, and I confess I was surprised myself to hear of it."

"And why was that?" I asked.

"When he first came here the boy seemed to have a true vocation. But so young he was, perhaps it was just a fancy on his part, for after he had been here a few months, something changed in it for him. And, as soon as he could, he ran away. Stole a coracle, he did, and fled back home—was it Kintyre he was coming from? It was just shortly after you came here, Muirteach, that all of that happened."

For myself, I did not remember the boy at all, but when I thought back on how trapped in my own misery I had been at that time, perhaps that was not to be wondered at.

The talk turned back to finding my father's killer. We both agreed that although Gillecristus had been back for Matins, he could still have found my father crossing the Strand a few hours before, killed him there, and gotten back in time for the service.

"But then why would my father have run towards the cross? I would think he would have been trying to run the other direction, had that been the case."

"But perhaps whoever murdered him hid on the shore, and attacked him as from behind as he crossed the Strand."

"Then it would not likely be someone from the Priory."

"That would be a blessing," Donal said.

I looked at him sharply, seeing him for a moment as if I did not know him. The man had spent most of his life here, at the Priory. He was devoted to it. Could Donal have killed my father for some reason, to protect the Priory? Or perhaps he schemed with Gillecristus? I shook my head. This search was making me a crazed *amadan*. Then I realized I had not told Donal of my vision.

I did tell him then, all of it, even the words of Muirreadch Albainnich that my father had quoted. Donal shook his thin face, crossed himself, and looked distressed.

" 'The sins a man does in secret,' " he mused. "Sure and your father had his share of sins, Muirteach."

"I am knowing that."

"Still, it is a sad thing he is not resting more quietly, now that we have buried him. We must be praying for his soul, I am thinking."

I agreed with that, and then realized the tide was turning, and unless I went quickly it would be a hard thing to take the boat back to Scalasaig. So I bid Donal good-bye and returned to the main island.

Pray for my father's soul, I thought to myself as I worked the oars. Now that is something I would never, just a few days ago, have ever imagined myself doing. And yet, the odd thing of it was, when Brother Donal had suggested it, I had agreed. I did not know if it was the vision I had had, or the wild beauty of the music the bard had played the night before at Aorig's, or what it was that caused it, but my hatred for my father slowly seemed to be transforming into something else. Shedding its skin, somehow, in the manner of a selkie, but what the new shape of it all would be I could not yet tell.

The fancy made me feel a little calmer, and I was able to put the need to find a killer—any killer—which His Lordship had impressed upon me when last we spoke, out of my mind for the time. I lost myself in the light spilling over the water, the feel of the oars, and the sun setting over the western sea in a blaze of glowing clouds as I rowed back to Scalasaig that evening.

But Mariota Beaton I could not put out of my mind so easily. She had returned to Islay, on some business of her own. Whyever should she not? And why should the thought of it rankle? Yet rankle it did, pricking against me like a nettle scratch, while I sailed home through that russet-and-gold-colored sea.

CHAPTER 12

After I beached the boat at Scalasaig I fetched Somerled from my house, then we climbed up Dun Evin to Uncle Gillespic's. It had grown late and the sun finished setting as we climbed up to the old hill-fort. Somerled, glad for the excursion, ran ahead of me, yelping excitedly, and then circling back to encourage me as I followed more slowly. The watch had lit the torches at the gate, against the night. I saw them glimmering brightly in the gloaming as I neared the top, my leg paining me, and my breath coming quickly after the climb.

I had hoped to find my uncle's household still eating the evening meal, and luckily enough, I was not disappointed. As I entered the hall the aromas of peat smoke, roasted venison, bannocks and Euluasaid's good ale swirled together, tantalizing me. I sniffed the air, and I realized how hungry I was. My aunt welcomed me, and grudgingly allowed Somerled to join the other dogs in the hall. They settled down, after the requisite sniffing and circling, before the fire. I sat down gladly on a bench near my uncle, and fell to with a will, not pausing to speak with Gillespic until my belly was full.

Over another *mether* of ale I told him what I had learned since last we had talked, of Tormod and of Calum, and of Sheena and her pregnancy. How Columbanus most likely would not have murdered his own sister. Of Gillecristus, his hatred of Sheena, and of his quarrel with my father before his death.

If I had hoped for great wisdom from my uncle I was to be

131

disappointed this evening. He leaned his back against the wall, for we were sitting on a bench at table still, and stroked the chestnut hairs of his beard as he listened to my story.

"So you are not thinking it is the Islay MacDonalds, then?" he asked.

"Whatever reason would they be having to kill Sheena—" I started to say indignantly, then I looked at my uncle again and discovered the twinkle hiding behind his eyes.

"No, now uncle," I answered then, more easily. "For whatever reason would they be having to come skulking here in the dead of night and killing my father, eighteen years too late, as it were? A cold revenge that would be. And even less reason would they have to be killing his leman. I am thinking the *each uisge* did it. It swam up onto the Strand and choked my father with his own bowstring."

I saw Aunt Euluasaid cross herself quickly when she heard my mention of the water horse. She claimed to have seen it once, swimming in a loch on the mainland, but for myself I was not certain that I believed her story.

"Excepting for the fact, of course, that my father did not have a bow with him that night."

"Aye, Crispinus was never one for the hunt," returned my uncle dryly, while my aunt shook her head at our levity.

"So you are no closer to knowing who has done this, Muirteach?" she asked, while she filled my glass of ale from a clay pitcher.

"Aunt, I have no notion. And it is not helping that himself on Islay is wanting it solved as quickly as ever might be, which means yesterday, or better still, last week."

"You will be finding the black-hearted one who did this to us, *mo chridhe*," my aunt said comfortingly, before she left us to our ale. "It is certain I am of it, knowing you as I do." A good woman was my aunt. Why she believed in my abilities to solve this puzzle, I did not know. It was my mother, not myself, who had had the Second Sight, and my mother was long dead.

"So you have no music tonight?" I asked Uncle Gillespic, after we had drunk the last of our ale.

"No, White Aengus is over at his sister's son's wedding for some days, and taking his harp with him. And the traveling bard has moved on, to Mull I think it was he said he was going to. Why the man wanders so, I cannot say, with the gift that he has, he could be the bard for His Lordship himself. But he does not bide in one place for long, he chooses to wander."

"What do you know of Tormod?" I asked my uncle after another swig of ale. "And of his kin? What of Calum? Is he a competent craftsman?"

My uncle thought a moment before he replied. "Young Tormod is headstrong, and always has been. He would be a bad man to have on the hunt with you. He would be shooting before the deer was there. And then the arrow would be hitting you, and he would say that someone else had the firing of it. Although I do not think the man would be limping all the miles down to the Strand to be killing your father, not now, when he can barely be leaving his bed to take a piss."

"Tormod told me he was injured the day before my father was murdered. But wasn't Alasdair Beag saying he had seen him crossing the Strand that night—"

"Surely the entire masons' village will not be mistaken about the day, nor would an entire village lie," my uncle replied. "Especially not for Tormod. He is a troublemaker, and that is a fact. Perhaps Alasdair got his days confused."

"Perhaps," I said doubtfully. Alasdair Beag was old, but he still had his wits. "He must have. But what of Tormod's kin? Are you thinking they would have done it for him?"

"Why not be killing Calum?" returned my uncle reasonably. "It makes no sense to be killing the Prior over that. It is Calum's responsibility, as head mason, to see that his workers are safe."

"And what of Calum? Is his work shoddy?"

"Och, no," said my uncle easily. "He has work aplenty in Kintyre, and Iona, and even some work in Edinburgh and Rothesay for the King. But he does like the drink, now and again. It is a failing among our men, that," he said, eyeing me where I sat sprawling against the wall of his hall.

I did not feel I could argue the point with my uncle, as the ale I had drunk seemed not to be helping my logic much, so I just asked him if I could spend the night in his hall. When he said yes, as I knew he would, I curled up on a bench with Somerled snoring next to me, and drifted off, watching the shadows the flame from the firepit cast on the rafters and the thatch.

CHAPTER 13

I lay on my mattress, trying to ignore the bracken that poked me, and stared at the blackened thatching, which formed my ceiling, through the dim afternoon light filtering in from the door. My mood matched the blackness of the thatch.

My investigation seemed at a dead end. Despite what Alasdair Beag had said, Tormod's injuries were such that he could not have moved from his bed when the killings took place, and I was beginning to believe that the old man had been mistaken. Gillecristus was not accounted for, but in truth, I really did not believe he had killed my father and then Sheena. Nor did I believe Columbanus would have killed his own sister. Angus and Alasdair also had alibis, for Rhodri and Malcolm had returned from Barra and had vouched for them.

And so my thoughts turned to the Islay MacDonalds. Perhaps after all they had killed my father. And perhaps I should visit Islay to discover what I could. That Mariota Beaton was on Islay also I dismissed as mere coincidence.

It did not help that my half brother, still at Aorig's, was playing a loud and unruly game outside. I surmised, from the sound of it all, that the boy was re-enacting the routing of the English at Bannockburn. He was hitting against the stone side of my humble home with some stick, and the noise of it did little to improve my mood. I heard Somerled barking furiously, it seemed Sean was chasing him, pretending the dog was a knight on a charger, or some such thing. Finally, my head pounding from the clamor, I went outside to intervene.

"Sean," I yelled at him, "you be stopping that now!"

My brother glanced at me briefly, then continued banging the stone corner of my house with his sword, a wooden stick, while Somerled barked loudly, just out of reach of the stick.

"You will be angering the dog. Stop it, Sean!"

It seemed my half brother was deaf, for all the racket he was making, for he continued to ignore me, and continued to pound on the wall. I suddenly found I was sore tempted to apply his own stick to the lad's bum.

Still, I did not. Instead, I walked over to him and took him by the shoulders. "Sean, stop it now. Were you not hearing me?"

From the glare he gave me I guessed that the boy had heard me well enough. I let go of his shoulders and stood facing him. "What is it you were doing?" I asked him.

"And why is it I should be telling you?" he asked, belligerently. I found myself thinking wryly that perhaps my younger half brother and I had more in common than I had suspected, from the tone of voice that he was using, and from the defiant look that was in the boy's eyes.

"You will be telling me because it is my house you were banging on, and it is my dog you were tormenting, and it is my head that is pounding because of all your noise."

"Nothing," he said, now looking at the dirt below his feet.

"Nothing?"

"Nothing, that is, I do not know. I was playing."

I waited, my anger changing to some sympathy for the lad. "Playing at what?" I finally asked. "The Battle of Bannockburn?"

The lad shook his head.

"What was it then? Whist, I am your brother, lad, you can tell me."

Sean kicked his bare foot in the dirt and would not look at

me. Now I was curious. "Sure it cannot be so terrible, whatever it was, for all that the clamor of it was giving me the headache."

He would not tell me, but at least looked up and seemed less afeared. "Yon's a big dog you have," he observed.

"Aye. He is named for our ancestor, Somerled. Are you knowing of him?"

Sean shook his head yes, for what boy here does not know of Somerled, who founded Clan Donald so long ago. "He was singing of it," he said.

"Who?"

"The harper."

I did not remember the bard singing of Somerled that night we had heard him at Aorig's, but he must have sung some more after I had left.

"And look," the lad continued. He reached in a grubby pouch he had tied around his waist and took out a harp-tuning pin. "It belonged to himself," he said.

Sure, it must be one of his boy's treasures, I thought, remembering my own small collection I had had at Uncle Gillespic's. A hawk feather, a crystal stone, a fairy bolt, and such things. I smiled at him.

"Well, and so he was giving it to you, then?"

Sean remained silent, which I took for assent, but he smiled a little at me. It occurred to me that I had not questioned him about the day his mother died. I had only questioned Maire. Perhaps the lad knew something of it all.

"Sean," I asked, "would you like to go walking with Somerled and myself? I can show you the old faerie-fort up the road a bit, the one on Beinn Nan Gudairean. Have you ever been there?" It would be a climb, but it was all worth it, I guessed. Especially if the boy knew anything of his mother's murder.

My half brother shook his head no.

"Would you like to go?"

Sean shook his head again, in the affirmative.

"Well then, we shall go. But not tonight, I am thinking," I added, for although the days were long this time of year by the time we walked to the beinn, climbed it and explored the fort, the sun would be setting in the west and it would be very late. "We shall go tomorrow."

"But you cannot climb—" said Sean, who then stopped himself quickly.

"Aye, yes I can so," I started to reassure him, but before the words were well out of my mouth, Maire emerged from Aorig's house. She seemed aye upset to see me there with her brother; her face was white and she shook somewhat as she stood in front of me. She grabbed her brother and pulled him away from me, back behind her. Somerled, who had quieted down when I was talking with Sean, began to bark again.

"Do not be talking with him!" she cried, her voice shrill.

"But Maire," interjected Sean, "he said he will be taking me to the fort. Tomorrow, he said."

Maire slapped her brother. "No, now, you will not be going—" Her thin shoulders heaved. Sean started to cry, then, from the blow and from seeing his sister in tears. Myself, I was totally confounded by it all.

"But, Maire," I asked, confused, "whatever is it?"

"You are not to be speaking with him! Not without that I am there. My mother said I was never to leave him alone!"

Just then Aorig, hearing the girl's cries, came outside, followed by Seamus. Her hands were wet and her face red.

"Why Maire, whatever is it?" she asked, echoing my own question.

"He," she said, pointing to Sean, "is not to be alone. My mother said so, she said I was to stay close by him, and not be leaving him alone, not alone with the men, and now he is wanting to take him to the fort. Tell him he cannot be going! It isn't right—he cannot go. Mother would not have wanted him to go!" She broke down into sobs.

Aorig looked at me apologetically. "She is having a hard time of it, Muirteach, what with her mother being gone." She drew Maire into her arms and stroked her back, soothing her. "Whist, white love, it is only Muirteach we are speaking of. Your brother will be safe enough with him, I am thinking."

"But Mother said he was to stay close to me. He was not to go alone!"

"Och, Maire, for sure your mother would not be minding. Muirteach is your brother, he is kin to you and to Sean."

"No," the girl said stubbornly. "She said he was not to go."

Aorig looked at me, her brow wrinkled with her puzzlement. "It is making no sense to me whatever, Muirteach. I am sorry about it all." The girl was completely hysterical, but at least her brother had stopped his crying.

"There, there love, you must stop your fretting and wailing," continued Aorig, attempting to calm Maire again. I was relieved to see that at least the girl's sobs seemed a little quieter. "Whatever it is, it can wait until tomorrow. We will be talking about it then, and not before. Come on back inside, there's a good girl. You too Sean, and I will be singing a song to you all and perhaps a wee bit of milk and honey, to send you to sleep, with the Saints to watch over the both of you and no more worries to be vexing you." She crossed herself and walked back into her house, with her arms around both children. Seamus remained outside.

"Whatever was that about?" I asked Seamus. "Is it making any sense to you, at all, then?"

Seamus shook his head, as mystified as I myself was. "She is an odd girl, that Maire," he observed. "She helps Ma, and takes care of the wee bairn, and sits, rocking him for hours on end. I am not knowing what it is to make of her, but Ma says that I must not be bothering her overmuch, for all that she has gone through."

I said nothing, but Maire's outburst rankled. For the one thing, she looked at me as if I was the *Ùruisg* himself, and yet I had done nothing to the girl that I knew of. What was it she said, he was not to go alone? Why not? What was to befall Sean if he did?

Och, there was no sense to it at all. Shrugging my shoulders, I went inside and got the flask of *uisgebeatha* I had, settled myself down on the bench outside my house, offered Seamus a drink, and then took more than one myself, while the clouds moved in and covered the sun.

The more I thought over Maire's behavior the more perplexed I grew. Sure and there was no understanding women, and Maire, for all that she was but a young girl, still fell into that category. I almost found myself wishing Mariota were here, to ask her what she thought of it all.

Still, I grew more determined to speak with Sean. Perhaps he and his sister knew more of their mother's murderer than they were telling. The girl had seemed fearful and her behavior had made me curious. So I went over to Aorig's hut the next morning, early, for all that I had a bit of a headache from the last night's *uisgebeatha*.

Maire was rocking the baby, while Aorig busied herself making the morning's porridge. Sean was helping her, bringing in some peats for the fire. He grinned at me, then quickly glanced at his sister.

"Good morning, Muirteach," Aorig said, smiling. "And is it that you are hungry this morning that we see you so early? Or is it your dog that you are bringing over here to eat my porridge?"

I worried that Maire would get upset again when she saw me, but she just looked up, stared at me, then went back to rocking her brother, crooning him some lullaby.

"Well, Aorig, I am fine this morning and thank you for asking. I would enjoy some of your fine porridge, if you can be sparing some for me."

Aorig glanced over at the girl and shrugged her shoulders, as if to indicate there was no telling what had ailed the lass the night before. As she handed me the wooden bowl of porridge she murmured, "I am still not knowing why she was so upset last night, Muirteach. She seems calm enough the now, but still, I am not liking it."

I was not liking it either, but it was Sean I wanted to speak with. I feared to mention another excursion to the faerie-fort, although I felt confident that Sean would have liked to go. But I kept silent on that, afraid it would lead to a repeat of the scene of the last evening.

I motioned to Aorig. "I am wanting to speak with Sean," I whispered. "Is there a chore or two he could be doing outside, where I could speak with him. I do not want to be upsetting his sister again."

Aorig nodded. After I had finished eating, along with Sean and Seamus, who had returned from taking the cows out to pasture, she said, "Sean, now, just you be going out and finding those nests the hens have made. I am needing some eggs, and I am thinking that you will be just the boy to be finding them for me. You can be feeding the hens as well." She handed him a willow basket for the eggs, and a bowl filled with feed and some scraps.

Sean nodded, obviously pleased with the chore. He seemed to have settled into life at Aorig's without a ripple. But Aorig had a way with children.

After a moment or two I got up, thanked her for the porridge, and went outside, along with Somerled. I found Sean, having finished feeding the hens, raiding their nests while they ate.

"Look, Muirteach, this is the fifth one I have found." He held up a fine large brown egg for my perusal.

"You have a fine pair of eyes in you, Sean," I told him.

"So will we be going to the fort today?" he asked me.

"Och, Sean, you were seeing how upset your sister got last evening, just at the thought of it. So I am thinking not now, at least not today. But perhaps we will go later when your sister is feeling better. Are you knowing why it is that she was so worried about it all?"

Sean shrugged his shoulders. He was a well-favored boy, with reddish hair like his mother and blue eyes. His cheeks were plastered with freckles.

"I am not knowing, Muirteach. Just that mother was never wanting me to be alone with himself when he came to visit, she was afeared I would be bothering him I am thinking, with my games."

"Are you speaking of your father?" *And mine too,* I thought.

"Aye." He nodded. "I was to sit quiet, or go away outside."

For sure, Sheena would not be wanting her children to be annoying their father. But children had been annoying their fathers since the dawn of time, and it seemed a little reason for the girl to be taking on so about it.

"But then, he was not coming to see us," Sean added with an adult practicality which surprised me. "Most times he came at night and we were supposed to lie still in our cots and sleep, when he was there."

"And did you?" I asked.

"Aye."

"Was he there often, at your house?"

Sean looked puzzled. "He did not come to visit every night, but often enough. And Mother said he was our father, and a churchman besides, and so we should greet him respectfully when he did come and we were not yet asleep. But most times we would already be in bed when he came to visit."

"Were you knowing, Sean, that he is my father as well?"

Sean looked uncomfortable. "I was hearing that he was your father, but I was not sure, as you are so old, I was not believing it."

"And how was he treating you?"

Sean beamed. "He was proud of me." As he was not of me, I thought, with a touch of bitterness. "He would pat me on the head and say I was a handsome, well-favored boy."

Well, all this was fine enough, and it was a pleasant enough conversation with my half brother that I was having, but it did not answer my questions.

"Are you remembering the night your father was killed, Sean?"

He looked puzzled. "The night before you came to visit us at our house, that day?"

"Och no, it would have been two nights before that day. Are you remembering that night?"

Sean nodded.

"Well then, was there anything unusual about that night? Did your father come to visit that evening?"

He nodded again. "Aye, he came, a little late he was. I am knowing because I was still awake, it being so light and all. But then Mother had said I must be getting into bed, that himself would be coming soon. And I was almost asleep before he did get there. But then he was aye angry when he came."

"Was he saying why he was late?"

"He was saying he met someone on the way. He did not like to be doing that," Sean added confidingly. "Mother said it was because he was of the Church and all. That is why he was always coming at night, I am thinking. So no one would see him in the dark. But it being summer and all, the night was not that dark."

"Did he say who it was that he was meeting?"

Sean shook his head no. "I was not hearing. But he was hitting my mother over it all."

I remembered Sheena's bruise. Had she had another lover? Is that why he hit her, and was that who had killed him? But then, why had that person killed Sheena?

Perhaps, my father being the man that he was, he had not needed a reason such as another lover to hit her. He may have hit her before, regardless. For my father had a lot of anger in him.

As I had, I suddenly realized. The anger I felt for him, the anger I felt about my leg. In that, I resembled my father.

But this realization, for all that it made me feel somewhat ashamed of myself, did not go far to solving the question at hand. While I had been mulling this over in my mind, my half brother had found another two eggs. He arranged them carefully in the basket while I asked him one more question.

"That day your mother had her accident," for that was all I could bear to call it to his face, "was there anything unusual about it, Sean? Did anyone come by who you did not know?"

"No." Sean shook his head decisively. "I would have seen if they had. For was not yourself just telling me what a sharp pair of eyes I have. Mother used to tell me that as well."

He looked as though he was going to cry for a moment, but then he bit his lip and stopped its trembling.

I felt cruel for continuing, but I remembered the pin Mariota had spoken of. "When she left that day, what was she wearing?"

Sean frowned.

"Perhaps you will be remembering, with those keen eyes of yours."

His brow wrinkled with the effort. "Well, she had her plaid, and her shift and tunic. Nothing out of ordinary I am thinking.

144

And a basket, for the rush flowers."

"Are you remembering that fine pin she had?"

"The silver one? With the birds on it?"

"That is the one. Was she wearing that, that day when she left?"

Sean screwed his blue eyes shut, trying to remember. "Mother is walking out the door," he said. "She called to Maire to watch the baby, that she would be back in a while to feed him but that she was going to pick the plants for the dyeing. She turned to me and told me to turn the peats and after I had done that to go and collect dulse from the beach. And that is the last thing she tells me. I am thinking she is wearing her fine pin because I can see the glint of it in the sun as she turns to go."

"You are having the fine eyes for sure," I praised him. "And a good mind to go with them. Do you know where your mother was getting such a pin from?"

He shook his head no. I guess speaking of his mother had made the boy feel his grief again, for he looked as though the tears were not far away. I was minded of when my own mother had died of the plague so long ago.

"Well, Sean," I promised quickly, hoping to distract him, "Aorig and I will be talking to your sister. And I am sure she will be letting us go to the faerie-fort before much longer. Perhaps Seamus will come too."

Sean's expression brightened and I sighed in relief. He idolized Seamus, who would good-naturedly carry the boy on his shoulders, seemingly without tiring. I could not do such things, not with my leg as it was. But I was learning that my friendship had other attractions, mainly, four-footed ones.

"And will Somerled come, too?" asked Sean.

"I am thinking that he will have to," I assured him solemnly. With that, satisfied, Sean took his basket of eggs inside to Aorig, and I was left to puzzle over what he had told me.

If Sheena had had a lover, who would it have been? I had no idea, nor did I have much idea whom to ask about it. If Mariota had been here, she would have been able to ferret out the information from someone. But Mariota had gone back to Islay.

For sure I could not be asking Angus and Alasdair who else their sister had been sleeping with, the two of them were angered enough with me already. Ever since I had found the body of their sister at Dun Cholla the two of them glowered at me over their drink at Donald Dubh's.

Perhaps Aorig had heard something, or perhaps she could glean something else from speaking with the children. For I, myself, did not think that young Maire would be telling me much, not after her ranting last night. What had gotten into the girl?

Perhaps the poor thing was just reacting to her mother's death. Although I felt a twinge of sympathy, I found myself wishing my half sister would stop regarding me as though I were the Ùruisg himself, come to snatch her brother away.

I resolved to ask Aorig about it, and see what she could tell me. But Aorig knew nothing, when I asked her later that day.

"Sheena kept herself to herself," she said, "living down there alone, as she did. So I am thinking that your father was wanting her close to the Priory. Poor love, she was not even that close to her own brothers' house." Aorig continued her weaving for a moment, thinking.

"So no, Muirteach, I am knowing nothing of other men," she finally continued, after winding some more yarn on her shuttle. "I would have been telling you, if I had known anything of it. I have heard nothing from the women here either, so I am doubting, if she had a lover, that it was a Colonsay man, at all, at all. Everyone knew she was the Prior's handfasted wife. I am not thinking any Colonsay man would be risking your father's temper over it all. And I am not thinking that your father would be needing such an excuse to hit her, either."

"You may be right," I agreed glumly. "But then whoever was it my father was seeing that night, before he got to her house?"

"I am not knowing, Muirteach. It could even have been Alasdair Beag, for all that, out digging oysters while the tide was low. For the sun was not setting until very late."

But Alasdair Beag had told me he had gone to sleep early that night. So I doubted that was whom my father had seen that night.

But if Sheena's lover had not been a Colonsay man, then who was it? Islay was the closest island, but that was a long way to go to meet a lover.

CHAPTER 14

I decided to go to Islay myself. It had been years since I had seen any of my Islay relations. Although in my soul I seriously doubted they had sailed across the sound, killed my father, and then returned to Islay with no one being the wiser for it all, I told myself I might as well go myself and check on it all.

Especially since, as each long summer day passed, it grew clearer and clearer to me that I had no idea who had done these murders. Perhaps Mariota had discovered something.

As for the possibility of running into His Lordship on Islay, I told myself that would be unlikely. The Lord of the Isles no doubt had other, weightier concerns. Although he had said he wanted to hear of my results soon, as yet, I had nothing to tell him. At least if he sent someone to look for me here, in Scalasaig, he would not be finding me.

So I borrowed a small *nabhaig* of Uncle Gillespic's, taking Seamus along for crew, and we set out for Islay. The day was fine and the sailing easy. I have always enjoyed sailing and the sense of freedom I feel in a small boat skimming over the waves, and the trip to Islay gave me pleasure.

We sailed around to the Rhinns, and landed in Kilchiaran, where my mother and I had lived. I still had uncles and a great-aunt there, although it had indeed been a long time since I had visited. Once my mother had died and I had been fostered at my uncle Gillespic's, I had not often returned there.

Truth to tell, we had to ask directions from some local girls mending fishing nets on the sand, it had been so long since I seen the place. The girls giggled and blushed, and directed us inland, towards the village. We headed towards my great-aunt Morag's cottage.

Great-aunt Morag sat spinning, on a bench outside her cottage. "And whoever is it then?" she wondered, as we approached her.

"Great-aunt, it is Muirteach. Seonaid's son."

"Eh, Muirteach." She put down her spindle and stood to meet us as we approached. It seemed to me that she had shrunk since last I had seen her. Perhaps she had in fact, for age does that to a woman. But sure enough it was that I myself had grown since the last time I had seen her, as a boy of eleven.

"Is it you indeed?" she wondered. "Let me look at you, lad. Come close, for my eyes are not what they once were."

I went nearer and Great-aunt Morag touched my cheeks with her hand. Her old skin felt papery and cool as she ran her fingers over my face, peering at me closely with clouded blue eyes.

"Sure, and we were thinking that the *each uisge* himself had been swallowing you, for all that we have heard of you these last years. You have grown, lad," she added. "I would not have been knowing it was you, although now I can see a bit of your mother in you. Aye, and the look of your father as well. He was a handsome man, indeed, when he stole your own sweet mother's heart away.

"But what is it you are doing here, the now? We were hearing, awhile back, that you had left the Priory. We hoped to see you then, but you were not coming home at that time."

"No, Auntie," I replied, surprised at how good it was to see the old woman. "I have been with Uncle Gillespic, on Colonsay. I scrive for him, when he is needing things written."

She smiled. "Och, and so you can be reading and writing then, Muirteach. It is a grand thing, the reading and writing."

It crossed my mind to tell her that it was all I could do, since I could not run like other men, but I gentled my tongue, and merely agreed with her, that indeed it was a fine thing.

"But now sit you down, and we must be getting you some refreshment." She called inside. "Eilidh, be bringing out some refreshment for your cousin Muirteach who is just coming. Some cheese, and milk, and some of the oatcakes from this morning."

And so my cousin brought us some refreshment, and we ate our fill. The milk was creamy, rich with the taste of the good grass of the Rhinns, the oatcakes still fresh and crumbly, fair melting on the tongue.

"And where are Uisdean and Dougall?" I asked, after eating my fill of the oatcakes. These were my uncles, whom I dimly remembered as teen-aged boys with little time to spare for their crippled nephew.

"Eh, they're away the now. Uisdean is with His Lordship for a time, and Dougall is away to Antrim, fighting for the Sweeneys. He was leaving Eilidh with me, for the company. I am thinking he is trying to save enough money for a bride-price. He is wanting to marry again. A girl from Kilchioman, it would be, that he is wanting to marry."

Eilidh listened silently. Dougall, my uncle, was her father. Her mother, Dougall's first wife, had died some twelve years back in childbirth, along with Eilidh's infant brother.

"Are you liking the girl?" I asked my cousin.

"Well enough," replied Eilidh, evasively, "but she is not that much older than I am myself."

"And how long have they been away?" I asked my aunt.

"Eh, Uisdean was leaving some two months ago, in April it was. And Dougall, well, he has been in Antrim since March. But whatever is it that is bringing you back to Kilchiaran at this time, then?"

"You were not hearing of it, then, Great-aunt?"

"Heard of what? It has been little enough the news we've heard here the past few weeks."

And so I told her and Eilidh of my father's death. Great-aunt Morag seemed suitably shocked, making horrified little murmurs and crossing herself, particularly when I came to the part about the Sanctuary Cross and Sheena's death.

"Eh, Muirteach," she said when I had finished the grisly tale, "sure and it is not surprised I am that your father should come to such an end. A godless man he was, for all that he was of the Church. And it is glad I am that someone finally revenged themselves on him. I am thinking your mother is resting more easily in her grave now, the white love."

From the little I remembered of my mother I felt sure she would not have approved of my father's death, but, for myself, despite my mixed feelings about the matter, I still felt some sympathy with Aunt Morag's point of view. I went on to tell her of Sheena's death.

"And wasn't she just no better than she should have been, the sly harlot."

"Well, whatever, Auntie, I am not thinking that either of them deserved to die in such a fashion," I finally said. "And himself in Finlaggan is not thinking so either, certainly not a prior of the Church. It will make trouble with the King in Edinburgh, and with the Holy Father himself, and surely he will not be wanting that."

My great-aunt grudgingly agreed that that was so.

"In fact," I continued, speaking with some sense of self-importance, "he is wanting me to solve the mystery."

"And so it was for that you were looking to know where Uis-dean and Dougall had gone? Shame on you, Muirteach, to be thinking of that at all." I felt abashed.

"There seems to be no one on Colonsay or on Oronsay who

could have done it, Auntie, so I thought at least to check here," I said, by way of excuse.

"Uisdean and Dougall were already young men when their sister, your mother, was put aside by that black-hearted snake. And I am not thinking they would be waiting until now to be taking revenge, if that is what they were going to do about it all. But they have done nothing about it, Muirteach, for what with your father being His Lordship's Prior and all, they were not wanting to get on the wrong side of himself."

"Aye," I agreed, in a sense relieved. Things could get quite touchy for my uncles if their clan chief was against them, especially if that chief happened to be the all-mighty Lord of the Isles. I had not seriously believed that my uncles would have taken all that upon themselves, all for a wayward older sister who had been too headstrong to keep herself out of trouble.

"Himself is aye anxious to have this affair solved," I continued after a minute, by way of making conversation. "He was sending his own physician, Fearchar Beaton, to help with it."

"I know the man," said my aunt. "A fine physician, he is indeed. Were you knowing, Muirteach, that when he travels a far way they are sending his medical book by land, or on another boat, so that it will not be getting lost if his ship founders in the sea?"

I had not known of that. He had not been bringing that text with him to Colonsay, I guessed. He had not come there to examine the living, after all.

"I hear they have land here in the Rhinns," I said.

"Aye, they do," said my aunt. Over the other side of Loch Gorm. In Balinaby, it is, near to the standing stone.

"What was the Beaton finding, when he looked at the corpse?" my aunt asked after a pause, her curiosity getting the better of her.

"It was a grisly murder, Auntie. Whoever killed him hit my

father on the head from behind, then strangled him with a bowstring. And then, finally, stuffed his mouth with sand from the Strand."

Eilidh had listened quietly to all this discussion. Finally she spoke. "I am knowing Mariota, the Beaton's daughter."

"Aye?" I asked. "Where are you knowing her from? Balinaby?"

Eilidh nodded, the brown plaits of her hair swinging a little with the motion. "She was here, a day or so hence, was she not, Auntie? But she did not speak of the murders, at all. She is to be married soon. To a MacNeill, it is. From Mull."

"Is that so?" I answered, trying to sound unconcerned. Mariota had not mentioned a betrothal, but then, I had not asked her. I told myself that I was surprised anyone was wanting to marry her, with that sharp tongue she had. But apparently someone did.

"And what was she wanting here?" I asked, although privately, I realized she had been investigating, as she had promised to do.

"Och, she was just visiting, that was the whole of it, Muirteach. We were speaking of women's concerns."

And that was all Eilidh or my aunt would say of that matter.

Seamus and I spent that night and the next day with my great-aunt. It was not possible, after not seeing my Islay relatives for so long, to leave abruptly. For my part, I enjoyed the time we spent there. There were no other close relations there to query. The plague had hit my mother's family hard, that same time that she herself had died, and so, after ascertaining that Uisdean or Dougall could not have committed the crime, I relaxed for a time, and basked in the loving attentions of my great-aunt. I felt unencumbered, freer than since before my father's murder, for all that I had not yet solved it.

And I am thinking that Seamus enjoyed his time on Islay as well. At least, it seemed he greatly enjoyed taking the time to flirt with Eilidh, as she went about her tasks. I heard him humming the words to "Nut-Brown Maiden" quietly when he thought I would not be hearing.

One thing nagged at my memory, and finally, the last afternoon of our visit, I remembered what it was.

"Were you knowing, Auntie, of a boy who went to the Priory a little before I did, and then did not like it, and left?"

My aunt's fingers never stopped picking the fleece she was preparing for carding, but her rheumy blue eyes took on a faraway look as she thought.

"An Islay boy, you are saying? How old would he be being?"

I tried to remember what Donal had said. "A bit older than myself. I am thinking he may have come from Islay, but perhaps he was not coming from the Rhinns."

"Wait now, Muirteach, I am remembering something. I am thinking that one of those MacKerrals from over near Kilchioman, sent a boy to the Priory a bit before you yourself were going there. It was a long time ago, but I am remembering because I was thinking, at the time, that perhaps the lad would prove to be company for you. Now was it a MacKerral? Or a MacCrimmon? Aye, I am thinking it would have been a MacKerral."

"From Kilchioman?" That was not so far away, after all, and on the way to Balinaby. Perhaps we would stop by there before returning to Colonsay.

"Was I not just saying as much?"

"Do you remember his mother's name?"

My aunt's fingers stopped picking the fleece a moment as she thought. "Alsoon was his mother. She was married to Iain, I am thinking. And they lived a way out from the village, not as far as Dun Chroisprig, but in that direction."

So it was that the next day we left Kilchiaran and sailed a bit up the coast, beaching the boat on the sands of Traigh Mhachir.

A young boy taking cattle to pasture was happy enough to point us in the direction of Alsoon and Iain's steading, which sat in the shadow of Dun Chroisprig, not too far from the end of the beach.

So intent were we on looking back at the beauty of Mhachir Bay, that we nearly missed the house. A tiny holding it was, the weathered gray stones of the walls of the house blending in so well with the stones on the green slopes of the hills, that we nearly walked past the place, until the noise and movement of a woman turning peats by the side of the house alerted us to the dwelling. She was an old woman, with gray strands of hair hanging down about her face. She wore no kerch and had a suspicious look to her eyes. Her clothing hung about her, somewhat ragged, and the wet peats had stained her hands and feet a dark brown.

"Who is it, then?" asked the woman.

Guessing that this might be Alsoon, I introduced myself as Morag's nephew. Alsoon knew of my aunt, and she invited us to sit down and refresh ourselves. The ale she served tasted somewhat sour on the tongue, but I drank all of it despite that, for the heat of the summer day.

"I am looking for your son," I finally said. "Is he here?"

Alsoon looked puzzled. "You are knowing my son?"

"I knew him long ago," I lied. "At the Priory on Oronsay."

The old woman spat on the ground. "Be away with you, then, if you are from that place."

"Mistress," I tried to calm her, "I left the place. Do you take me for a monk?"

"You do not have the look of the monks," she grudgingly admitted, after a moment.

"When were you last seeing your son?" I asked. "What became of him?"

"Och, he stops now and again, when he is in the area. But he has the wanderlust in him, he does, and someday he will leave and when he returns I will be in the ground, with never a son to mourn at my wake or wrap me in my shroud. But he was just here, oh, a week or so ago, it was."

"And how long was he staying?"

"For a few days. Then he was away again. What are you wanting him for?" she asked, her voice suspicious.

"I am wanting to speak with him. Can you tell me where did he go?"

"You are not knowing him at all, are you?" she suddenly turned and stared at me, her eyes sharp and hard. "Whyever are you looking for him, then? And to think I was giving you drink, and all—get yourselves gone from here," she sputtered. "I'll be telling you no more of him!"

CHAPTER 15

After that dismissal Seamus and I sailed a bit further up the coast to Balinaby, around Carn Mor, and beached the small boat on Saligo Bay. We then walked the short distance inland to Balinaby, past the old standing stone. The old abbey of the culdees had been abandoned after the Norse raids, and now the Beatons held the land. It was easy to find the Beaton's house, surrounded as it was by a fine herb garden. A grand enough house it looked to be, the garden enclosed by a low stone wall, the thatch neatly held down and all in fine order. I wondered if Mariota remained here, or if she had gone back to Finlaggan.

We found out soon enough, for of a sudden someone stood up from behind the wall. Mariota had been weeding, apparently, for her skirts were kilted up around her waist, revealing her pretty calves, and her hands were full of some plant or another. She wiped her hands on her apron and greeted us. She smiled, and I grinned foolishly in return to see her there.

"Muirteach—whatever is it that is bringing you here to Islay? And Seamus—"

"I had it in my mind to visit my relatives here for myself, to see where they were during the murders," I muttered, suddenly self-conscious.

She nodded. "Aye, and were finding out just what I did. Your uncles were away and could not have been doing it."

"Well, why were you not sending word and saving me the

trip, then? And why did you not mention the murders to my aunt?"

She smiled a little. "Perhaps I was wishing to see you, Muirteach. But if you have already been on the island here with your relatives for two or three days, how are you to know I was not sending you word? 'Tis you who are the impatient one."

"And how can I not be," I retorted, "with himself breathing down my back like MacPhee's black dog, to be solving this matter?"

"Speaking of dogs," she retorted, with the sunlight shining on the gold of her hair, "where is Somerled? Were you leaving that great dog of yours at home, then, Muirteach?"

Seamus, totally ignored by the both of us, pretended interest in the lavender patch and some comfrey, while Mariota and I glared at each other a moment. Then she laughed her silvery laugh, and said, "Come away in then, the both of you, and I will get you some refreshment."

"And so are you alone here? Where is your father?" I asked, after she had settled us with a cool glass of barley water, herbed with lemon balm, spiced and sweetened with honey. Although I told myself I would have preferred claret, the sweet coolness of the drink was refreshing on the hot day. And there was no denying it quenched the thirst.

"My father is away at Finlaggan. But my aunt bides here, with my cousin. For someone must stay to mind the garden, Muirteach. It does not weed itself, you know. She is away this afternoon, at a birth up towards Ardnave. It is a first baby and I am not thinking we will be seeing my aunt until tomorrow. Robbie is away fishing. He will be back when the shadows lengthen."

I wanted to ask her about her betrothal to the nameless Mac-Neill that Eilidh had spoken of, but I did not. For it was no business of mine, after all, if the daughter of the Beaton went and got herself married. Marry she should, I thought sourly, and soon, for otherwise she is like to become an old maid. At least that MacNeill would take her.

My thoughts troubled me, and I busied my mind looking around the room. There was a fine large table under the window that served as a desk, from the look of it. On it were piled papers and many books. More books rested on a shelf nearby; the whole family of the Beatons looked to be rare ones for the reading.

I walked over and examined them, *The Odyssey*, and other works of the ancient Greeks, intrigued me. They sat beside other books, medical treatises mostly, among them *De Re Medicina*, and the *Lilium Medicinae*. At the time those works had little meaning to me, although now I know them somewhat better.

Bunches of herbs hung from the rafters to dry and gave the house a sweet, grassy smell. The beaten floor was covered with rushes. All seemed in neat order. As I looked at a small wooden cupboard hanging from the whitewashed wall I realized Mariota was asking me something. "What was it you were saying?" I asked.

Mariota made a little face. "You are wearied, Muirteach, that is plain enough. I was asking what news there was from Colonsay. What else have you been finding out, since I was last there?"

I told her. After all the dead ends we had found here on Islay, I was more and more of the mind that it was Gillecristus who had done these things. Which would not be making me a popular man with His Lordship, at all.

"Where is himself these days?" I asked.

"Why? Do you have news for him?" asked Mariota.

I shrugged my shoulders, as though I did not care, but felt a fear deep in my gut. "I have no idea who has done these murders. Unless it was Gillecristus. Have you seen His Lordship? Was he asking about it, then?"

"He mentioned it to my father."

"And what was your father telling him?"

She smiled, her blue eyes twinkling a bit. "Och, my father told him of the second murder, and how that had made the whole situation here all the more complicated."

"And?"

"Himself has some other things to be thinking of the now. He is after the Earl of Ross, to betroth his daughter to young Donald, but I was hearing that things are not going well with that."

"Is not Donald still with the King?" I asked, relieved at the thought that His Lordship had something else to occupy him for the now. For His Lordship's son, Donald, had been in Edinburgh for some years, a hostage for his father's good behavior to the Scottish Crown.

"Och, he is still there. But the word was that he might be returning soon."

Bleakly, I wondered if the MacLeods of Lewis had need of a scribe, for it seemed unlikely that I would be welcome in His Lordship's territory after all was over. Or perhaps I could get work in Edinburgh, at the court, or even in England.

"Are you knowing that MacKerral woman living over at Kilchioman?"

"Aye," nodded Mariota.

"She was aye unfriendly to us. I am thinking her son went to the Priory as a boy, but he left the place. She did not wish to speak of him, at all."

Mariota nodded again. "She has her ways, does Alsoon. Her humors are sadly out of balance, but she wants no help from any healer. She stays alone there, and I fear she broods. I am thinking that, when I was younger, she was not so. But her husband cut his hand on a scythe, just a small cut it was, but he died within two days. My father tried, but he could not stop the poison in the man's blood. Since that time poor Alsoon has not been so well in her mind. My aunt will be knowing her better. You must be asking her about it all."

There was a pause, I felt my head nod, and she suddenly said, "Look you, Muirteach, you are tired. Why do you not rest yourself in here the while, and I will just finish weeding that bit of speedwell, and that meadowsweet, before the afternoon is gone. Then we will be eating, if Robbie is bringing some fish back. And I think that he will, sea trout most likely it will be. For you both will be hungry. Seamus, if you are not tired, why do you not come and help me out here."

Seamus complied, and I leaned my back against the wall where I sat, breathing in the sweet scent of the herbs. They must have been hops, some of them, for I could not keep my eyelids from closing, and I let sleep overtake me for a time in the heat of the afternoon.

I had a strange dream. Mariota was there, on some high place, and she held something in her hand, with that smile of hers on her face. But when I walked closer to see what it was, she laughed, and changed into a bird, a kestrel it was, and flew away. I could see whatever it was she had been holding, still glittering in her talons.

As it was a dream I followed her, beating my own wings, for I too had become a hawk, flying out and over, over the Sound of Islay and on across to Oronsay. We could see the seals swimming in the shallow waters and sunning themselves on the beach; even the young seal pups with their mothers in the sheltered cove where they whelped. Fantastic it was, that we could see every detail of the shoreline of Oronsay.

How fine it was to move so freely! Being as it was a dream, our flight made no sound and I felt no wind on my limbs. We flew over Sheena's cottage, which looked dark and abandoned from its point over the sound and continued across the Strand.

The tides were out, and on the Strand red dulse, kelp, and yellow bladderwrack shone wetly on the white sands and glistening dark rocks. But we kept flying, over the path leading to the Priory until at length we hovered over it. The masons worked on the North Range. I could clearly see Padraic and Moloug out in the fields and sure, I was even seeing the beehives set out, the wicker of them yellow against the green of the plants in the gardens.

The sun, brighter than the brightest flame, was heading towards its bed in the western sky, and of a sudden, in the air before me, I saw the glint of its rays on whatever it was that Mariota had been holding. The glittering object plummeted like a rock, down, and I felt myself descending with it, the green grass inside the cloisters coming up to meet me at a fast rate. This is it, I thought, and braced myself for the fall.

I jerked awake.

I was still in the Beaton's house. The shadows had lengthened some across the floor and the room felt close with the summer heat filling it. My neck was stiff from the odd way I had leaned it against the wall, and my bad leg sore from the walking we had done that day.

I had dreamed, that was all of it. I found myself wishing for some claret, and shook myself to shake the dream away, even as I regretted the lost beauty of that flight. It brought to mind the wild notes of some elusive song, the sound of it fading out of reach even as I tried to grasp it.

But what was it, I thought, that Mariota had been holding? The silvery glint of it came back into my mind's eye—that brooch, it must have been, falling to the Priory. And perhaps all it was meaning was that my father had given it to Sheena, indeed, and that was the message of it then. But where was that brooch now, and who was the killer?

The door opened and a gangly youth entered, with a small creel of trout. "You will be Muirteach, I am thinking," he said easily. "I am Robbie. Herself was telling me to be quiet when I came in here, but now you are awake."

"Aye." My throat was dry. "Is there something to wet my throat with? I am parched."

Robbie nodded, and filled a beaker with some claret from a jug, then one for himself. I drank thirstily, and was just setting it down on the kitchen table when the door opened again and Mariota entered, along with Seamus. She carried a basketful of young nettles, and after a greeting, proceeded to busy herself with the food, frying some bacon in a pan, then adding the trout while my stomach let me know, insistently, that I had not eaten since leaving my great-aunt's.

All the while she kept up a chatter with her cousin and Seamus, about nothing in particular, while I nursed another beaker of claret, feeling strangely surly and uncommunicative, the searing beauty of my dream lost in the bustle of the evening.

The food was good, but I fear I did not thank her for it. I left the pleasantries to Seamus, who ate almost everything in sight, and complimented Mariota effusively on her cooking. I took myself outside after the meal was over, and watched the sun set behind the standing stones of Balinaby.

The next morning I asked Mariota again about Alsoon Mac-Kerral, and at length Mariota agreed that she would go and try to get more information from Alsoon than I had been able to. Seamus and I prepared to return to Colonsay, having accomplished our purpose here on Islay—ruling out my relatives as suspects in the murder. So there was nothing for it then, but to return home.

We walked down to the beach, where we had left our small boat. The wind was brisk, with white clouds scudding across an azure sky, and the wind was in our favor. The trip to Colonsay promised to be a quick one. We said our good-byes, and Seamus pushed the boat into the sea, then jumped in, while I raised the sail. The golden sands of Saligo Bay grew more distant as we prepared to continue on up the coastline, before crossing the eight miles or so of open sea between Islay and Colonsay. I was glad the wind made rowing unnecessary that day, although I have strong arms and shoulders and can row well if need be.

We rounded the rocky western corner of the island. The black rocks glistened against the gray waves of the sea. The breeze grew more blustery, and I feared a gale. The wind stiffened and I noticed Seamus, who had been working the bailing bucket while I tended to the sails, working faster at his task.

"Look you, Muirteach," he cried, trying to make his voice louder over the sound of the wind, "she is filling up with water very fast. I am not liking it at all."

I looked at my feet and the water was reaching my ankles, in fact, it seemed to be pouring into the boat far too quickly. I surveyed the boat, my eyes moving quickly due to my anxiety, and saw the reason.

Someone had bored some small holes in the hull of our boat, and stuffed them with tallow. But the tallow had been washed away by the action of the waves against it, and now water poured into the boat, not only from the odd wave that washed over the gunnels—an expected part of sailing—but also from the holes in the hull.

Someone had wished us ill and wanted our boat to sink.

Someone had taken advantage of our overnight stay at Balinaby, to drill those holes. The boat, lying on the beach without a guard, had been an easy target. And now Seamus and I, fool that I was, would pay a high price for my carelessness.

I cursed myself for an *amadan*, but that did not help our situation, and the depth of the water inside our boat was increasing. It sat lower in the waves with every passing moment.

"Seamus, keep bailing," I ordered. I did not need to. Seamus, his face white, sensed the gravity of our situation, and worked doubly fast to get the waters out of the boat, while the first drops of rain from the squall pelted us in the face. I secured the sail and joined him, frantically bailing with another pail.

Who had done this to us? How easy it would have been, sometime during the night, for someone to drill the holes and then plug them with tallow. We would sink, in the sound, with none the wiser for it. But who? And why?

The waters rose in the boat and the stiff wind pushed us past *Eilean Bean* and towards Nave Island. Perhaps, if the boat sank, as it looked to do very soon, we could save ourselves and somehow get to Nave Island. If the boat sank further out in the open water between Islay and Colonsay there would be no saving us at all.

I explained my plan to Seamus, while I turned the rudder to steer us into the island.

"Muirteach," he cried, "I cannot swim."

Indeed, most island men cannot. We are lovers of boats, not swimmers like the seals, for all they say the MacPhees are descended from those selkies. However I had learned to swim as a young child. I believe some doctor—probably the Beaton himself or one of his family—had recommended it, telling my mother it might strengthen my legs. And the skill had proved of use, from time to time, when things had fallen overboard or other such happenings occurred.

"It does not matter, Seamus," I told him with more confidence than I felt. "You will just be grabbing onto some of the planking and I will swim us both into the shore. You can kick a bit, to help us along. Do you understand me? Do not let go of the planking and keep me in your sight. If we lose each other when the ship goes down, you must find me and holler if you are not seeing me right away. I will find you."

The water was up to our knees at this time, and I stopped bailing, it being of no use, and busied myself those last few seconds with throwing the rowing benches overboard in the hopes that they would float so that Seamus could be grabbing onto one.

The rocks of Nave Island were almost past us and I began to fear we would not be making them. If we missed them there were only the tiny Balach Rocks to the north before the open sea of the channel. I grabbed the rudder again and gave one last tug on it, turning the boat sharply toward the Na Peileirean, and of a sudden I heard a loud crack as the mast broke off and crashed down into the water, missing Seamus by just a few feet. His face was white and I saw his lips moving in a prayer, although I could not hear what words he said, as the water came rushing over the gunnels and the boat finally broke apart and went down.

I caught a glimpse of Seamus, overcome by a white wave crashing over the deck, and I shouted to him, then started stroking the water with my arms, trying to swim towards him as the boat fell away from under my feet and the water engulfed us.

CHAPTER 16

It seemed a lifetime before I found Seamus, although in reality it could only have been a moment or two. He held onto the fallen mast like a barnacle, his head just above the waters and his hands white with the effort of his grip. The rain was coming down in earnest now and the waves were choppy as I joined him in grabbing onto his mast.

"Seamus," I managed to say between gulping for air, "hold on tight, and I will swim us to shore."

He nodded without speaking, his eyes large in the angles of his face.

I glanced around and could see the rocks of Nave Island. The tide had turned and was now coming in, and I thought that perhaps, with luck, it might bring us into the shore. I managed to position myself alongside Seamus and held onto the mast with one arm while I pulled with the other. I kicked the water as well, but I have never had a strong kick when swimming.

"Seamus, kick your legs. There, yes," I encouraged him as he began to kick. And slowly we began to move towards the shore.

The tide helped us, and at the last, the rocks of the north side of the island came towards us with a rush and I feared we would be crushed. But somehow we clambered onto the slippery rocks, and then clambered a little higher, out of the reach of the waves, until like seals we sat shivering on the highest point and looked westward, where our boat had been, but we saw no trace of it in the gray waves.

Shivering, we watched the gray sheets of rain fall on the choppy waters, and then the squall passed away towards westward and a pale sun came out. We roused ourselves, clambered up the rocks to the grassy top of Nave Island, and headed towards the chapel.

It is said that Nave Island used to be home to some of the culdees, and even that Saint Adamnan lived there long ago, but, for myself, I can think of no setting less hospitable. Perhaps that is what they were wanting, those early priests. The island, for all that it is not far from the main land of Islay, has an air of remoteness about it. At least it did so on that day, as Seamus and I made our way towards the tiny chapel visible on the eastern edge of the island.

It was slow going. My bad leg cramped, and I could hear the sound of Seamus's teeth clattering together as he shivered. I did not know anything of the island and simply prayed that someone was at the chapel who would see to us. For succor we badly needed that day, such water rats as we were.

The chapel was a small gray stone building, which sat on the edge of the island, looking over a promontory towards Gortan-taoid Point on the main island. It blended in well against the rocks and water behind it, so that it was almost invisible. As we approached we could see two or three small houses near the chapel; one would be the priest's, I surmised. Perhaps the others belonged to fishermen, although why anyone would live on such a cold and dreary place I could not fathom.

An older man wearing the robes of a priest looked up from the garden he had been tilling. "Whatever is it, then?" he asked, a quizzical expression on his weathered face. Briefly I explained, leaving out the bit about the sabotage. Let him think us incompetent sailors if he must. Best not to give too much away, I thought, not sure myself why I was not so forthcoming.

"Well then, you first must be getting warm," said the man

practically. He led us into his house, sat us before the peat fire, and gave us a drink of *uisgebeatha* mixed with hot water, as well as some porridge, which helped to stop Seamus's teeth from clattering so and brought a bit of color back into his cheeks. The lad still coughed now and again, and I did not like the look of him.

"You will be wanting to sleep, I am thinking," said our benefactor, whose name was Father Padraic. "And then tomorrow we will be seeing about getting you back to Colonsay. Perhaps one of the fishermen will be taking you over, if not to Colonsay, at least to the main island and you can be hiring a boat from there."

I nodded, suddenly too exhausted to puzzle it all out, and thankfully laid myself down on the pile of bracken the priest provided, covered myself with a woolen plaid, and sank into a profound sleep.

When I awoke the next morning I could see that the sun, its beams shining in through the narrow slit window, had already risen high in the sky. I looked for Seamus but did not see him and wandered outside to find him.

Seamus was helping Father Padraic with his gardening. He looked much better, thankfully; the recuperative powers of the young I supposed. I was feeling much better as well. The sky was clear today and the sea calm, and Nave Island looked much more pleasant, with the little wildflowers blooming in the machair here and there, and white clouds, like young lambs, frolicking in the blue sky overhead. Father Padraic looked up and greeted me.

"And so you are awakened after all. It is a sound sleep you were having, and no mistake."

I nodded, and wondered about a boat back to the main island. "Who is it that lives here with you?" I asked.

The old man nodded with his chin towards the other small huts. "There is Iain Mor, the fisherman, and his brother Niall Sgadan. He is called so because he is such a great one for the fishing of herrings, is Niall," added the priest by way of explanation.

"And do they have a boat? Would they be taking us to Islay, or even over to Colonsay?"

"They will take you to the main island with no trouble, I am thinking," said Padraic. "As for Colonsay, they might be taking you there if there was something in it for them."

I nodded, but my few coins had been lost in the wreck and so I doubted we would be getting a lift to Colonsay with Iain and Niall.

"And no one else lives here?" I asked.

Padraic nodded his head no. "Their mother passed away last winter. A dreadful cough she had, before the end. And their father was lost at sea some years ago. They are bachelors. They have no wives to do for them, but I am thinking they will be finding some before much longer."

"There are no other people on the island?" Seamus stopped his weeding and looked curiously at me but I had my reasons for asking.

"Och, we get the odd visitor now and again, and some poor wounded beings in need of solitude and healing, but no one else makes their home here." A gannet cried overhead, emphasizing the isolation of the spot.

"So now tell me of yourselves," Padraic continued after a moment. "What was bringing you here to Islay? And how did your boat happen to go down yesterday? The weather was not as bad as all that."

I said we had been visiting relatives on the Rhinns, to bring them the news of my father's death. As for the boat, I just said it had sprung a bad leak, one that we had not been able to plug.

Seamus shot me a confused look, and I sent him a telling look back, hoping he would not contradict me. The story was true, as far as it went.

Padraic nodded. "Well," he said, "Iain and Niall are out away in their boats the now, taking advantage of this fine day. You must be waiting until they return, and then you can be asking them about it all."

We helped Padraic with his gardening awhile longer, and then he went into the chapel to say Mass. We followed, and the three of us were the only celebrants. The chapel had a peaceful feel to it, and I was surprised to find the service brought some calm to my soul. Perhaps the Lord would help me to find my father's killer, I mused as the Mass ended, for I myself was making a fine hash of it all.

We shared Padraic's simple noonday meal of cheese and bannocks, and then I said I had a mind to explore the rest of the island.

"It will not be taking you long, I think," observed Padraic dryly, "but sure and it will give you a chance to be stretching your legs." So Seamus and I set off.

"Why were you not telling him about the holes in the boat?" asked Seamus. I told him my reasons and we explored the island. There was a small hut towards the southern end, by the beach, with a small boat pulled up onto the white sands.

"Who is living there, do you think?" asked Seamus.

"I do not know," I answered. "Perhaps it is a fisherman's hut."

We did not intrude and quickly ended our circuit of the small island at the chapel and Padraic's own house. The island was small, as he had said, and it took little time to walk around it.

Padraic greeted us, then said, "Iain Mor and Niall are back. You can be asking them about the boat, if you want."

We walked down the machair to the house Padraic indicated,

a low, long, stone dwelling, thatched, with one door for both beast and man. Although we saw few beasts there. Iain and Niall, being fishermen, kept but one cow. A tall man, whom I guessed to be Iain for his height, was driving it into the byre as we approached.

I explained our request and he nodded. "Come away in then, and we shall speak of it."

He ushered us in, and offered us some *uisgebeatha*, then sat, nodding over his mazer while we explained again what we wanted. Outside I heard voices, his brother Niall, I guessed, and another voice, lower, which I could not catch; it must have been Padraic.

"I am not knowing about Colonsay," Iain Mor finally said. "There is a good run of fish on the now. We are not wanting to miss them, for they fair jump into our nets. But we will be taking them over to the main island—the day after next, it is, for the market. You can be going with us then."

It was not what I wanted to hear but perhaps it was all that we would be getting. "What of your brother?" I asked. "Would he be willing to take us over before then?"

"I am needing him to help with the nets," replied Iain.

"Who is living in that small hut on the end of the island?" I asked. "I saw a small boat there this morning. Perhaps they could be taking us over, at least to the main island."

Iain looked uncomfortable. "That is just an old boat, I am thinking. There is not likely to be anyone staying there the now."

"Who lives there?" I pressed.

"Och, it is just someone from the mainland. They are staying there from time to time, when they are traveling. They will be leaving their cows here for the pasture, that is all of it."

So at length it was agreed that we would ride over to Islay with Iain and Niall and their fish the day after tomorrow, when they went to market. I did not feel resigned to yet another day of inactivity, but neither did I feel like swimming to the main island.

The second day passed much as the first had, but at last the third day, market day, arrived, and Iain and Niall took us with them to the mainland—a trifling distance, really, but far enough if one had no boat. Once at the market in Kilnave, it was easy enough to find someone willing to carry us over to Colonsay, especially when His Lordship's name was mentioned. And so, some five days after we had left, we returned to Scalasaig, alas, without my uncle's small boat. But my dog greeted me with enthusiasm, while Uncle Gillespic took the loss of his boat philosophically.

"It is a sign you are getting close to the black heart of the matter, Muirteach," he said, as we walked up to Dun Evin in the evening after I had returned. "And whoever is at that heart is not wanting you to get any further. Who would that be, I wonder? That old woman, do you think she did it?"

"She would have had to walk some distance to find our boat. But that daughter of the Beaton was saying her humors are out of balance, and that she is daft. So perhaps she drilled the holes in the boat out of spite. I can think of no one else there who might have done such a deed."

There was another thing I had wondered at, and so I returned to the Priory early the next day, to speak with Brother Donal.

"Are you knowing of Father Padraic, the priest who lives over on Nave Island?" I asked him.

"I have heard of him, Muirteach, but he does not come here and I do not leave the Priory often. So no, I do not know him. But I have heard he is a kindly man and a good priest. He is an Islay man, himself, born and bred in the Rhinns I think it was."

"And who is his parish?"

"He is more of a hermit than a priest of a parish, on that

173

little rock. Some fishermen bide there, that is all."

That accorded with my time on Nave Island. I did not tell Donal of our wreck, I only said that I had been to Islay to visit my mother's kin, and had seen the island on our way back, and been curious about it.

"And what is happening here?"

"Calum is acting strangely. He is always checking the scaffolding like a mother hen, and he and Gillecristus are at each other like hounds. He is saying that Gillecristus is wanting the work done too quickly, that he is rushing the construction, while Gillecristus is saying that Calum is out only for the money he and his masons will be making if the work lasts longer."

Construction had been going on at the Priory for as long as I could remember and it did not seem likely to me that Calum would be needing to make the work last even longer. It had been at least ten years since His Lordship had endowed the latest construction, the cloisters, and the new church, and work had not stopped on them since then.

"And Columbanus?" I asked.

"He is the same. He bakes his bread, but now with such a mournful, sour and sad look to him that I am wondering how the bread is as good as it is. He cries during the Mass, grieving for his poor sister I am guessing."

"Have you heard aught of Tormod?" I asked.

"We have not seen him here at the Priory," said Donal. "He has not been back to work yet, although I have heard he is walking again. Thanks be to Our Lord."

"Aye," I muttered, with less enthusiasm. I had found young Tormod to be a singularly unlikable fellow. And perhaps not honest either.

I left Donal and found the masons. As the sun had climbed high in the sky they had stopped working and sat among piled stones, eating their noonday meal. I greeted Calum and explained whom I needed to speak with, and he pointed me to an area where some younger lads sat, chewing on bannocks and white cheese.

A gangly boy, a few years younger than Seamus by the look of him, looked warily at me as I approached them and asked for Eogain, Tormod's brother.

"I am he," he said. The lad was tall and sharp-featured like his brother. "You are Muirteach, are you not? The man looking into the murders for His Lordship?"

I agreed that indeed I was.

"What were you wanting?"

"I was speaking with your brother a while back, and was needing to ask you a few questions, that is all."

Eogain's eyes did not loose the suspicious look to them, but he consented to stretch his legs with me a bit and answer my questions.

"There is just one thing that I am wondering. Alasdair Beag was saying he had seen your brother down on the Strand, the evening that the Prior was murdered there. Yet that was the day your brother had his fall, so I am thinking he could not have been there. Unless he was not so injured as we thought."

Eogain flushed and ground an unoffending clump of wildflowers into the dirt while he looked at the ground.

"I am not thinking he could have been walking that day," he finally said. "We carried him back to Kilchattan the next day on a litter."

"But Alasdair Beag is certain it was your brother. He recognized the cloak."

Eogain remained silent.

"Surely you are knowing where your brother was that afternoon," I pressed. "Calum told me you stayed behind at the masons' village to tend to him, after the accident, when the other men had gone back to work."

"Aye, so I did."

"Well, could he move from his bed or no, that afternoon?"
Eogain shook his head.

"How was it then that Alasdair was seeing him down on the
Strand? If you are knowing anything of it, you must tell me
Eogain."

Another clump of flowers vanished under the boy's foot.

"His Lordship is needing this solved. If it was not your
brother, who was it down there that Alasdair saw?"

"It was myself," the boy finally admitted.

"What were you doing?"

"Fishing." The boy flushed scarlet again and kept his eyes on
the dirt beneath his feet.

"What is the shame in that?" I asked.

Eogain shook his head. "He had often boasted of it. Of what
there was on the far side of the Strand, how fine it was there.
And so I took his cloak and went, after he had fallen asleep."

"Is it the fishing you are speaking of?"

The lad nodded, but still did not look up.

"Well that is not so bad, is it? Were you catching any fish?"

Eogain shook his head no and finally met my gaze. "I was
supposed to stay and watch him," he said stubbornly.

"Well, and so you were, but if your brother was sleeping I do
not wonder you wanted to be out and away." I wondered at the
boy's reaction, for surely there was nothing so shameful in bor-
rowing a cloak and going fishing. "How long were you gone?"

"Not so long as all that. I went down to the Strand and
returned before the masons quit for the evening."

He glanced to where the other workers were standing, preparing to resume their labor. "I must go back, they are starting
again." I nodded my consent and the boy sped back like a rabbit towards the construction.

★ ★ ★ ★ ★

I returned to Colonsay, and found Seamus waiting for me eagerly at my house.

"They are saying," he announced, "that Sheena had a lover."

"Who is saying it? And who are they saying it was?"

"All of the women. I heard my mother speaking of it with Donald Dubh's wife."

"What were they saying?"

"Just that she must have had a lover who killed her. For"— Seamus frowned a little—"some of them are saying she was with child. So they are thinking her lover killed her for that."

Well, this gossip accorded with my own suspicions. And the women who laid her out would have known of the pregnancy. "Did you hear anything else?" I asked Seamus. "Were they saying who it was?"

Seamus shook his head. "Just then she was after me to finish turning the peats, and I had to pretend I had not heard what they were speaking of."

"Well, what of Maire and Sean? Was your mother asking them about it at all?"

Seamus shook his head. "No. Ma was shaking her head when she left Donald Dubh's wife, saying that they were foolish wives to be gossiping so, about a poor woman in her grave. Then she told me to keep quiet about it around the poor bairns, so I am not thinking that she would be speaking with them about it at all, at all."

"No, I do not think so," I agreed. "But I may just be asking her about it all."

Chapter 17

I found Aorig hard at work by the butter churn, while the baby slept nearby. Maire and Sean were not there, off with the cows, Aorig told me.

"It is just as well they are not here, Aorig, for there is something I wanted to ask you." I told her what Seamus had reported. "Are you thinking it is true?" I asked her. "For if it is, whoever it was could have killed her, if she was to bear his child and he did not want the fact known."

As I said the words I thought again of Gillecristus. Hard as it was to imagine him fathering a child, I could easily imagine him killing to prevent the child from being born.

"Och, I am thinking it is just the gossip, Muirteach." Aorig stopped churning a second to wipe the sweat off her forehead, then went back to her churning. "The butter is just coming in," she explained, "I cannot stop the now."

I watched her work, and picked a blade of grass, chewing on it while I waited.

"I am not knowing who it could have been, Muirteach," she continued, after a few more minutes of churning. "I am thinking there is nothing to it, myself. Sheena kept herself to herself. She was not so friendly with the other women, and people were not that kind to the poor lass."

"But don't you see, Aorig, it fits. Perhaps her lover met my father, and killed him out of jealousy, then for some reason killed Sheena when she told him she was with child."

"Well, if a man is jealous enough to kill, I would be thinking he would not be killing the object of his desire so quickly."

"Unless she threatened to tell what she had seen, if she saw the first murder. Or if he did not want her to have the child."

Aorig looked troubled, and frowned a little. "Such wickedness as that would be," she said. "Well, I still am not knowing who it could be."

"Still," I persisted, "Maire and Sean must know, if the person came to the cottage. I could speak with them about it."

Finally Aorig relented. "If you must. But do not be upsetting that Maire. I had the devil's own time getting her to sleep after you upset her that last time."

I confess I was afraid to speak with Maire again. My half sister unnerved me, with those sad eyes of hers, and after her last outburst I felt even less comfortable with the lass. So instead I went to Scalasaig, to Donald Dubh's, to drink some claret and to speak with his wife.

I started on my second beaker of wine before I went to find her out in the brew-house. Inside the walls were neatly whitewashed and all looked clean and tidy, as she tended to her ale. The small building smelled of yeast and of barley, not unpleasant, and Donald Dubh's wife herself was pretty enough to look at, with rosy cheeks and her kerch spotless white.

"And so, Muirteach, what can I be helping you with, then?" she asked. "You are not usually a one for the ale, and I see you have a full mazer of wine, so that cannot be why you are seeking me out here."

"I was hearing that you were thinking Sheena had a lover. I was wondering who you were thinking it might have been."

An unpleasant glint appeared in the woman's green eyes. "Och, Muirteach, I am not knowing, not for sure. People were saying that perhaps it was Tormod, from Kilchattan, the same one that was injured. They were saying that your father told

Calum to cheat on the scaffolding, to save time, and that Calum did so for blood's sake, seeing as the Prior was family, and that Tormod fell, and that Sheena herself was killing your father out of revenge for it."

"Well, so that is what they are saying," I said. "And who would be saying all of this? What reason do they have to say it?"

"Well, one of the women from near the chapel down in the glen was saying she had heard from her man, who also is over on Oronsay, working on the new construction, that he had seen Tormod walking towards Sheena's often enough before he took his fall."

That accorded with what Alasdair Beag had told me, but I did not mention this to Donald's wife.

"There are others that live in that same area."

Donald's wife shook her head emphatically. "None so many, Muirteach. And why should he be walking in that direction at all?"

"Perhaps he was just wanting to stretch his legs, after a day at work," I suggested. "Or maybe he liked to fish, and took himself over to the water there."

"Fish for something else, more like," returned Donald's wife.

"How could Tormod be killing her, what with his injuries from the fall and all that?"

"I have heard he is doing much better. And perhaps he was not as injured as he let people think. That mother of his, she worships him, for all that she barely lets him wipe his own bum. She would do or say whatever he told her to."

"Still, it seems little enough to be concocting such a theory."

"Well, then, Muirteach," she returned, "are you knowing who did kill her? And who killed the Prior? I am done here," she said, putting the cover back on the barrels of ale. "Will you come in and have another mazer? I see you have drained this one dry."

"I will think on what you are saying," I told her finally. "As for the mazer, I will not take it now, as there is someone else I must be speaking with today. But I will be seeing you soon enough, and I will drink it then."

"Aye, Muirteach," she said, "you are not a stranger here. We will be seeing you, I am sure of that."

I left gladly. There was something about that woman that I misliked. Perhaps it was the glint in her eyes when she spoke of poor Sheena, as though she could not wait to find fault with the woman, for all that she had never harmed Donald's wife.

Sheena had had few friends among the women here I was learning; she had lived as an outcast out there near Beinn Eibhne. And she had been an imposing woman for all that, caring little what people in the village said of her, and attractive enough to create jealousy among other women. I saw again Sheena's body in my mind's eye, lying there in Dun Cholla. She had not deserved the death she had received, nor had my father, whatever he had done.

So perhaps Sheena's lover had killed my father, and then killed her, once he had found out she was pregnant. Or because she had seen him kill the Prior. But the question still remained, who was Sheena's lover? Was it Tormod, as Donald's wife suggested? My father was not one to suffer rivals, in any arena.

I resolved to speak again with Tormod. Perhaps he would let slip something. I went without Seamus this time, as he was once more cutting the peat and I did not wish to wait. I borrowed a pony from my uncle and rode the distance to Kilchattan more quickly, arriving at Tormod's in the early afternoon. He looked much improved, sitting out in the front of his mother's cottage.

"Tormod," I said, "how are you faring?"

The man still showed a sour expression on his face, but

whether it was from pain or from dislike of me I could not be telling. "Well enough, Muirteach," he answered. "And what is it that is bringing you to Kilchattan today?"

"My neighbor Aorig was wanting me to check on you and see how you were getting along," I lied. "And it being such a fine day and all, I thought to escape the peats. I left Seamus to work them."

I thought I saw a flicker of a smile cross his face.

"I was also bringing some *uisgebeatha*. Are you wanting some?"

This time there was no mistaking the smile. I dismounted and secured the pony—a fine gray, one of my uncle's—sat down next to Tormod, and opened my flask.

"My mother is away with the sheep," said Tormod. "So she will not be back until the evening."

"A fine thing indeed that is," I replied. "But how is it you are getting along, with that sore hand of yours?"

"Och, it is not so bad the now. But I still cannot grasp the hammer. I must bide here, but my mother is seeing to me."

A black-haired young woman with a pocked face came walking back from the bay to her cottage across the path, and glared at us, sitting there taking our ease in the bright afternoon, before she spread some washing out to dry on some nearby gorse bushes.

"Do not be minding Giorsal," muttered Tormod. "She has a look on her that would sour milk. I am thinking she does not like to see me drinking so early in the day."

"And what is it to her?" I asked.

"She is wanting to wed me." Tormod took another swig from the flask. "But I am not of a mind to be marrying her, not with that look that she has."

I muttered something sympathetic, inwardly rejoicing that the conversation had taken such a turn so early. "And is there anyone you would be wanting to wed?" I asked. "Or have you stayed clear of such traps?"

"I am not wanting to wed. A wife and bairns, squalling all the day—and with my hand as it is, how could I be thinking of it at all?"

"What was the Beaton saying of it all?"

"He is thinking it will heal. He says I must be patient." Tormod spat on the ground then took another swallow of *uisge-beatha*. "But I am thinking it will never be like it was, and that Calum Glas will be paying for what he has done to me."

Tormod's lip curled upwards in an unpleasant smile, which made me glad I was not Calum.

Giorsal, who had been lingering in front of her cottage, finally went inside. A few minutes later, however, she emerged with her spindle and sat down on a stool outside.

"Let us be going around to the back," I suggested. "Surely there is a place we can drink without her watching us like the hawk."

Tormod agreed that that would be the thing. He rose easily enough and led us behind his mother's cottage to a large stone that overlooked the small bay. "Aye, this is better," he said, as he eased himself down on the seat.

"You are walking more easily now," I observed. Tormod nodded. "So you were hearing about the woman Sheena," I continued, passing the flask back to Tormod.

"Aye," he replied. "They were saying, Muirteach, that you were finding the body."

"That I was," I replied. "It was inside Dun Cholla, that I found her. She is leaving three bairns, Tormod. They are staying with Aorig the now. And were you knowing, the women who laid her out were saying she was pregnant again."

"No," Tormod replied. "I was not knowing that. I did not know the woman, myself."

"She was a fine woman to look at, with that height, and that red hair she had."

"Och, she was a bitch, I am thinking. The Prior's whore, she was."

"But perhaps pleasant to bed, for all that. She had a lusty look to her. Did she take other lovers, are you knowing?"

Tormod took another drink but said nothing.

"Some of the women were saying they used to see you walking towards Beinn Eibhne. They were thinking you were Sheena's lover."

Tormod laughed. "There is some good fishing over on that side of the island. That is why I walked there. And it was not so far from the masons' village on Oronsay, and not that hard to cross the Strand in that small coracle that they keep there. I could get away from the noise and the dust."

"But were you ever seeing Sheena, when you went there to fish?"

"Yes, I was seeing her. A strange one she was, and no mistake. She was often out on the heath, wandering. I am not knowing what she was doing with her bairns."

"So she would go alone? You never saw others with her?"

"No." The drink had affected Tormod now, as it had myself, although I had tried not to drink overmuch. He now leaned towards me.

"Were you knowing, Muirteach, I was not telling you the truth, not entirely."

"Oh?"

"I was walking to fish one day, and she was there on the beach. She had been gathering shellfish, I am thinking, but she had taken off her shift and was in the water, for it was a hot day. She thought no one could see her. She was a fine woman, with the large hips on her."

"What did you do?"

"I hid behind the rocks, and I watched for a while. She came out, and spread out her mantle on the sand, and then laid herself down upon it to dry in the sun. Her hair was shining like a river of bronze in the light. Like a selkie, she looked, there, the fine hips of her and her white breasts spread out sunning in the warmth of the day. The nipples of them, so pink and round they were, I yearned to suckle on them like a child."

I said nothing, repelled, yet excited despite myself, at his speech.

"Och, it is a fine woman she was, Muirteach," Tormod said. The drink was in him and he was not watching his tongue. I listened, like a rabbit entranced by an adder, while he continued.

"The thighs of her, and where they came together, the fine garden that was there. A feast for the eyes, it was, and I grew hard to see her there. After a time, she slept."

"And you?"

Tormod flushed red, took another drink, and then spat on the ground. "I spilled my seed onto the black stones, watching her from behind the rock there, and then I left the place."

CHAPTER 18

"Och it is a sad, sad thing it is, Muirteach, to think of that beauty lying dead and cold in the earth," continued Tormod, after another swig of the whiskey.

"Did you ever see her again, like that?" I asked. "Sure and it is no wonder you were going there to fish."

And it was no wonder, I thought to myself, that Eogain had shown such shame when he spoke of it as well. No doubt he had not gone down to the Strand to fish but to spy on Sheena himself.

"Aye," Tormod replied. "She did not come every day, but she did sometimes, and I would hide and watch her. Sometimes I would come in the evenings, after the work was over."

"Aye, Alasdair Beag was saying he saw you walking there often. He even swears he saw you going that way the day Prior Crispinus was murdered. But I was thinking that was the day you fell from the scaffolding, and how could you be walking there that day?"

"Och, no my arm hurt so badly that I just lay in that small house in the masons' village the whole afternoon, for it was not until the next day that my mother brought me home. I slept all that day, I am thinking it was the medicine they were giving me, for the pain of it, that made me sleep."

"But you had told your brother of it, did you not?"

Tormod nodded.

"So I am thinking perhaps he borrowed your cloak that day

and went down to the Strand himself."

"He was back when I woke up, fixing some broth," insisted Tormod, and that agreed with what Eogain had told me.

Tormod's eyes filled with tears. "How did she die, Muirteach?"

"You are not knowing, then?"

"I have heard dreadful things, Muirteach. I have heard they gutted her like a fish. It is a sad thing that, to think of that white belly—"

Either Tormod was a good dissembler or else he truly was not knowing how Sheena had died. "No, Tormod, she was not cut with a knife," I interrupted before he could go on. "She was strangled."

"Ah." He sighed then, a long deep breath. When he spoke again, his voice was hard, all the drink gone out of it. "Find her killer, Muirteach, find the black-hearted *nathrach* and I will cut his heart out with my own dirk. I will bleed him like the cattle are bled in the winter, and I will drink his blood."

Tormod's mother returned home shortly after that, and I soon left to ride back to Dun Evin, troubled by what I had heard. Tormod, for all his nastiness, seemed genuinely to mourn Sheena. I did not know whether of not he was speaking the truth when he said he had not lain with her, and he had said he wanted no bairns. But I did not think he had the courage in him to kill a prior, or Sheena, for all of his fine talk. I found myself satisfied, now, that it had been Eogain, not Tormod, that Alasdair Beag had seen that evening.

Which left Gillecristus, as unlikely as that seemed. Surely Maire or Sean would have known if their mother had regular visits from someone, not the Prior. So, whether Aorig liked it or no, I had to speak with them again. Perhaps the expedition to the fort of the *sithichean* would yield a chance to speak with

Sean, away from Maire. Or perhaps Maire herself would speak with me, without hysterics, now that some time had passed since her poor mother's death.

Aorig, providentially, was away at her sister's and had taken Maire with her when I arrived back in Scalasaig, and I found Sean out behind the byre trying to ride my dog. Somerled took it all in good humor, perhaps for the bits of old bannock which Sean was bribing him with.

"Charge," Sean ordered his steed, who instead wriggled around to bite at his own tail, dumping his rider to the ground in the process. The noble steed then nosed his rider, licking him in the face, while Sean struggled to sit up. I whistled, and Somerled left his tormentor and came to me, followed closely by Sean.

"I was thinking," I told Sean, "that tomorrow might be just the day to go to the faerie-fort. Are you wanting to go?"

Sean beamed. "But what of my sister?" he asked at length.

"I will speak with her. Perhaps she can go along as well."

Sean looked less pleased at this news. "She is a girl." He scowled. "Forts are for the men."

"Well, that may well be, but I am thinking that she will not be wanting you to come along unless she goes herself. And we can bring Somerled, too."

Sean, mollified at this, began asking me questions about the fort, who had built it, and when, all questions I did not know the answers to. And thus, when Aorig returned in the twilight, she found me with my half brother, a map drawn in the dirt of the yard of the island, with the fort marked on it.

"Maire," Sean called. "He is saying he will take us to the fort tomorrow!"

Maire looked less pleased than her brother at the news but she did not protest. Aorig looked dubious. "I am just thinking, Muirteach, that I might be coming along with you when you go, just in case." She glanced significantly at the girl. "I am thinking it would be a good idea."

"Aye," I agreed gratefully. "Perhaps we should all go."

And so it was that early the next morning Aorig, Maire, Seamus, Sean and myself set out for Dun Gallain. None knew who had lived there, the fort had been there past all memory, but it was sure enough that the Norse raiders had tried to storm it, when they took the Isles, but their weapons did not work there for the fort was of the faerie. I had found there, as a child, a faerie knife blade of worked flint buried in the dirt floor. It was said that no iron could be found in the fort, as it still belonged to the faerie, and that if someone unknowing brought the iron into the dun it would be the worse for him. And so we were all careful to have no iron on us when we went to the fort that morning, although we had fresh bannocks baked by Aorig and some fresh cheese with us.

It was a fine day, with the sky blue, with wisps of white clouds strewn across it like fleece from some giant spindle. The wind blew briskly, making it cooler than usual for the summer day. As it was some distance to the dun I had borrowed two horses from my uncle, one for myself and one for Seamus, while Aorig had taken their one horse. Her husband had declared his intention to hunt all the day, but Seamus had wished to visit the fort and his father had not gainsaid him.

I sat Sean before me on my horse and Maire, her eyes wide with it all, sat with Aorig and held the baby. Somerled loped along beside us, and we were a merry party as we rode along, like some chief with his retainers. Aorig told the children stories of the *sithichean,* the one of the hunter and the fairy flax, that gave his wife an easy birth, and then she told the story of the faerie husband, who had spent just one night under the hill with a beautiful faerie queen. When he returned to the world of men, he found that seven long years had passed away. Then we sang the song of the squirrels and the three little mavises, and before we well knew it the journey had passed, along with the sun climbing higher into the sky, and we were arrived at Dun Gallain. We tethered the horses at the bottom and climbed up to the dun.

A fine fort it still is, sitting on the rocks overlooking the Western Sea. An oval wall encloses a large area, and in some parts one can see the outer wall still standing as well. I sat down to take my breath, and rest my leg a bit, for the muscles of the bad one were quivering with the climb. Sean flopped himself down on the grass like a young puppy while Maire sat quietly next to Aorig, and at length I told the children a story.

"It is said the faerie stole a giant away, in the early days of the Dal Riata, when the world was still so young that the dew had not yet melted from the grass, and that this giant was kept in Fingal's cave, over on the island of Staffa. Kept in chains he was, by faerie magic, until he roared so that the *sithichean* swore they would release him after he had built them a fine fort. And this is the fort that he built for them."

"A fine big fort it is, too," piped up Sean. "But what were they needing it for, if they were the faerie?"

"Och," I replied, thinking madly, "why they were needing it for protection from the *cailleach*, the old hag that comes down from the northern mountains in the winter, with the snow swirling out of her white hair."

"Muirteach," said Aorig, a worried look on her brow, "you will be frightening the bairns, with your tales."

I ignored her and continued with my storytelling.

"And then, after he was finished, his chains fell away, for all that the *sithichean* do not always keep their promises, they were keeping this one for the size of him, and they knew they could not be holding him forever, giant that he was. And so, as his chains fell away, as he was putting the last stone into place, he dove away into the sea, and swam away, and was never seen again on the land. But the faerie cursed him as he swam away and the magic of their chains grabbed onto him again, and held him at the bottom of the sea. It is said that he lives still in the Cailleach, between Scarba and Jura, just over there," I finished, gesturing back in the direction of Jura. "He thrashes his legs, and kicks his feet to try and free himself, and that is what makes the whirlpool."

Maire's eyes were wide with the story, while Sean danced around in excitement. Even their baby brother, whom Aorig had brought along for the ride, laughed and kicked his feet at the clouds from where he lay on his blanket on the grassy hill. And after we ate our bannocks and our white cheese we entered the realm of the *sithichean*.

Inside, the walls kept the sun away, and it felt cooler, as if a cloud had obscured the sun, although when I looked up it was shining bright enough. Some smaller stone walls stood in the interior, dividing the space up into some dwelling places, I imagined. I kicked at the dirt and found a small fragment of black pottery, incised with faerie markings of a diamond shape, but I put it down and crossed myself. Just then Sean came running over saying he had found an elf-bolt. He showed it to me, a small point of finely chiseled flint, before he put it away in the pouch where he kept his treasures.

Aorig looked uncomfortable, and the baby began to fret while Maire stood over at the western wall, staring at the sea with an intensity I found somewhat unnerving. After a bit I walked over to her and stood beside her, watching the gannets swoop over the waves. One dived into the waters for a fish while we watched it.

"And what is it you are thinking, lass?" I asked her after a time.

She did not look at me, but kept her eyes fastened on the

waves, which pounded on the rocky beach below us. "I was thinking of Mother," she finally said.

"Maire," I said, "you are knowing who His Lordship is, are you not?"

"I have never seen him, but I am knowing he is a most powerful chief. Our father was always talking to my mother about him and all. He it is who set up our father at the Priory there."

"You have the right of it, Maire," I replied. "And himself it is who is wanting me to find the person that killed your mother—and your father as well. He is wanting to see that justice is done about it all."

"I do not care about justice. I just want Mother back again."

I felt the tears in my eyes while I thought what to say to her. The sea itself gave me the answer I needed.

"Och, white love, she is waiting for you in Tir Nan Og, the land of Youth, at the end of this very western ocean it is, they say. And after you have grown, and had your own wee bairns to mother, and then grown old with the mothering of them, then finally you will go and meet her there one day, a long, long time from now that will be. But I am thinking it would be making her very sad if she was to see you there anytime soon."

Maire said nothing, thinking on what I had said, I guessed.

"White love," I continued, "I am needing your help. Is there anything you can be telling me, anyone you might think of who had reason to harm your mother?"

Maire shook her head.

"And who would come to your house to visit there? Angus and Alasdair, your uncles?"

Maire nodded yes.

"And anyone else?"

"Just my father. But he said little to me, although he liked speaking with Sean. You came once."

"Aye, so I did. No one else?"

She shook her head no, but the movement seemed to have some doubt to it.

"Sometimes at night I would hear my mother talking and singing," she finally admitted. "And then I would think I heard another voice, a man's voice, answering her back, and I would hear music as well."

"It was not your father's voice?" I asked.

Maire shook her head no. "Father's voice was not like this one. This voice was like the rippling of the burn in the hills, so sweet it was. But when I would ask her of it she always told me I had been dreaming of the *sithichean* singing, or that she had been crooning a lullaby to him."

She nodded her pointy chin towards where her brother lay, sleeping quietly now. As if he sensed the movement in his dreams he stirred a bit and whimpered in his sleep. Aorig went to him and picked him up, then joined us by the wall.

"It is an ungodly place, this is," whispered Aorig to me, and I heard her say a charm under her breath. "Have you children finished exploring?" she called out in a louder voice. "For we had best be getting back home now, before the sun is going down entirely. There are still the cattle to be seen to, as you are knowing well enough, Seamus."

Even Seamus assented and only Sean seemed reluctant to leave the place. For myself, I felt eager to leave. The murders had cast a cloud over even this place that had been my refuge as a boy.

When we reached Scalasaig it was already late. Aorig's husband was back from the hunt, and hungry, and her family busied themselves with the evening chores of their holding. I wandered down toward the sea, accompanied by Somerled, picked up some pebbles on the stony beach and idly cast them into the water while I tried to piece together the puzzle. The ripples from one stone spread out, until they intersected another circular pattern, all orderly, unlike my own puzzle.

Somerled, tired after the day's excursion, did not even chase after the stones but curled up next to the large rock where I sat and left me to my thoughts.

It did seem certain now that the voice Maire had heard had been Sheena's secret lover. Whoever he was, most likely he had killed my father and then slain her as well, because she had seen the first murder or perhaps because of the child she was to bear. A fine tangle of mixed motives and black-hearted deeds it was, to kill one man for jealousy of a woman and then to kill the woman as well. But human hearts were full of evil, and stranger things indeed had happened in the world.

The late evening sun shone on the sails of a galley as it came into the small harbor from the direction of Islay. I watched, idly, as the boat grew closer and closer to the shore. The sailors jumped into the water when the boat was close in, and pulled it up onto the beach, set up the gangplank and unloaded their cargo and passengers, one of whom, I realized with glad surprise, was Mariota. It put lightness in my heart to see her, but I wondered why she was alone.

The noise of the unloading woke Somerled, and he barked excitedly at the sailors. Mariota turned her head at the noise, smiled when she saw me, and quickly walked over the rocky shore towards me.

"Och, Muirteach, and how were you knowing I was coming?"

"I was not knowing," I protested, "I was just sitting here watching the bay when all of a sudden here is this galley from Islay with you yourself on it."

"Well, whyever it is that you are here I am glad of it," she said, and at the words my heart gave a little jump, like the deer the moment it jumps over the rocks before it bounds away.

"What was your father saying, about you coming alone?" I asked.

"He was not knowing. He was away at Finlaggan and I came on." She laughed, and the sound of it felt sweet to my ears, as sweet as the golden honey of the bees of Saint Brigit.

"But should you not have a woman with you, for the sake of your reputation?"

"Muirteach, I could not be waiting for him to come with me, and there was no one at Balinaby to accompany me, so I came alone. My father will understand, when I explain. And I myself will guard my reputation, I'm thinking." The laugh went out of her face and she drew closer, speaking in a low tone of voice, "I have found the pin—"

"On Islay?" Several of the sailors turned to look oddly at me. I had spoken more loudly than I knew.

"Be quiet, Muirteach, and I will be telling you. Are you wanting all these men to hear of it? Let us leave this beach, and go someplace where no one is about and I will tell you."

So Somerled and I waited while she fetched her bundle from the ship, and then we set off walking, in the general direction of the village. But we turned and walked up by the cairn and the small stone circle, past the town, myself fighting my impatience with every step that we took.

Finally she stopped and turned, and drew something from her pouch.

"Look, Muirteach. Is this not it?"

I looked and indeed it was Sheena's pin. There was no mistaking the engraving around the outer circle, the design of strange birds interspersed with circles of knotwork on it, or the smoky cairngorm on it, catching the dying light of the day in its smoldering depths. And the blood, stained and dried in the silver carvings.

"Where did you find it?" I asked.

"On Alsoon's corpse. She opened her own wrists with it."

CHAPTER 19

"But where was she getting it? And why did she kill herself?"

"It is an awful thing, Muirteach, and a tragic one. But as for where she got it, I am thinking her son came and left it with her."

Some of the tangled threads of a sudden formed an interlacing pattern in my mind, clear and orderly at last. The harp pin little Sean had saved so carefully. The other voice Maire had heard, sweet like the singing of the *sithichean*.

"The bard. He must be Alsoon's son. And Sheena's lover. He killed Sheena, and took her pin."

"Yes."

"But Mariota—he could not have killed my father."

Mariota looked puzzled. "Why not?"

"Are you not remembering the day you and your father came to Colonsay with me, the day after himself had told me to solve the murder. The bard rode with us in the boat to Colonsay. So he must have been on Islay when my father was murdered, as well. He would not have had the time to return to Finlaggan so quickly, I am thinking."

"Perhaps not. Although with a boat of his own, he could have returned to Islay before you arrived. You did not leave for Islay until late that morning, that day after your father was killed."

"But why?"

"Jealousy perhaps? Over Sheena?"

"Then why kill her?" That part of it still made no sense to me.

"Perhaps Sheena was not so happy with what he had done. She did grieve for your father, Muirteach. Mayhap Sheena threatened to betray the bard, and then he killed her to protect himself."

"But then why did Alsoon kill herself?" My blood ran cold in my own veins at the thought of what the crazed old woman had done.

"That I am not knowing," said Mariota. "She was not right in her head. She claimed to hear voices, and often said she heard her husband coming for her. Perhaps she went to join him."

"What of her son?"

"I am not knowing when he was there, or when he left her, or why she would do such a thing, such a sad sin as it is. But she did kill herself. It was clear to see from the way the cuts were placed and how the blood ran.

"All I am knowing for sure is that one of the neighbors went by her house, to complain that her cow had gotten into his corn, and found her there, inside. So when I was summoned to look to the body, I recognized the pin. She held it in her own hands, stiff as they were."

"When did all this happen?"

"Her body was found the day before yesterday. The burial was yesterday and it was not until today that I was able to find a ship coming from the Rhinns to Colonsay. I did not want to send word, but wanted to tell you of it myself. And so here I am."

"Where is her son the now?"

"I am not knowing. None of us were knowing that he ever came to see his mother at all, we had not seen him for some years. Her cottage is isolated, and you can beach a boat on that wee beach there and make your way to Alsoon's house with no one being the wiser. Sometimes she would talk about her son, but none of the villagers thought she was speaking the truth. It had been so long since any there had seen him."

"And where has he gone?"

"We are not knowing that either. He is not at Finlaggan, and I am not thinking he is on Islay at all."

"When he left Colonsay he was speaking of going towards Mull."

"Well," said Mariota, all efficiency, "it should not be too difficult to find out if he took passage on a boat from here to Mull, or if he went to Islay first."

Mariota paused. "We are knowing he must have killed Sheena, to have brought the pin to his mother. We must find the harper, Muirteach. The two deaths are related, Alsoon's and Sheena's."

"Fine I am knowing that," I returned sourly. "Where are you suggesting that we be looking first?"

"Robbie is searching for him on Islay, with some of the other men. They had found nothing when I left. I am thinking perhaps he would go on to Mull. He was speaking of the MacLean of Duart, was he not? The one that married His Lordship's daughter?"

"Aye."

"Well then," Mariota returned, "we must get a galley. You can be seeing to that, Muirteach, while I check on those poor bairns of Sheena's staying with Aorig. I am thinking we had best leave as early tomorrow as the sun is up."

"Aye," I said again, resigned, for there was no reasoning with her. In fact, I grudgingly admitted to myself that she was probably right. And so, while Mariota walked briskly to Aorig's I trudged up Dun Evin in the twilight to see Gillespic about the galley and the crew.

We set sail early the next morning, on my uncle's smaller, six-oared *birlinn,* with some of the Colonsay men for crew and a fine wind to speed us to Mull. It was not long, a few hours only, before we saw the tower house MacLean of Duart had built atop the ancient foundations to house his fine bride, the daughter of His Lordship.

There was a fine story that went with that, for Lachlan Mac-Lean had kidnapped His Lordship himself and held him there until the man agreed to marry his daughter to the MacLean, only about six years past, it had been. A fine love match it was, and for all that himself had been wanting his daughter Mary married elsewhere, the two lovers had their way in the end, and were getting dispensation from the Holy Father himself in Rome to allow their wedding.

I thought to tell Mariota of the story, for most women love a fine romantic tale like that, but then I decided against it. Surely she knew of the tale, for all the Isles had heard the story when it had happened six years earlier. And, at any rate, was not she herself promised to some MacNeill? Let him tell her romantic tales, like some French troubadour of foreign courts.

Duart Castle stands at the end of the Black Point, on a high crag at the end of a peninsula which oversees the Sound of Mull, where it meets the Firth of Lorne, Loch Linnhe, and even Loch Etive. A fine strategic site it is, indeed, and a beacon lit there can be seen miles away, even at Dunollie Castle near Oban on the mainland.

So I am thinking it was no wonder that His Lordship had assented, finally, to the marriage, in order to keep the MacLeans on the good side of him. And the whole affair had had the advantage of killing off the Chief of the MacKinnons, so that the MacLeans now held almost the whole of Mull, as himself was giving those lands to his daughter for her dowry.

Well, whatever the outcome of that match had been, we had other business here the now. We drew closer to the rocky beach and disembarked at the stone jetty, explaining to the sentries posted there our business. There were other boats moored there, a small one that I thought I had seen before, and the MacLean's own galleys. Then we climbed the rocky path leading to the entrance of the keep. I showed my letter to the sentries, who were suitably unimpressed as they could not read it, but they let us enter once they knew we were from His Lordship.

The great hall of the keep had high timbered ceilings, brightly painted, and a large fire burned on the hearth. It took some time for my eyes to adjust to the smoky darkness inside. There were some fine tapestries on the walls, and obviously Lachlan Lubanach MacLean had spared no expense in fitting out this hall for his wife. I saw a woman, speaking with some other women by the looms set up in front of the narrow slit windows, and from the fine bearing she had, and the great pin she was wearing, I took her to be the wife of the MacLean.

Mary MacDonald MacLean was a tall woman, with large dark eyes set in a thin face. She had the look of her father in her, but somewhat of her mother as well, I guessed, that Amie MacRuairi whom His Lordship had set aside when he married the daughter of the King. I could not see her hair for the white kerch she wore, but her eyebrows were dark. She walked forward briskly to greet us.

"Mariota! Is it indeed you!"

The two women embraced like sisters and I was left wondering. But I should have known the two would have known each other, both being from Islay, for all that Mary was some years older than Mariota.

"Welcome," she said after we had introduced ourselves. "And what is bringing you to Mull today?"

"We are needing to speak with your husband. It is a matter of some urgency," I replied.

She raised those fine eyebrows of hers a bit, but asked no questions, although she must have wondered what her childhood friend was doing here in the company of these Colonsay men. She merely told us that her husband was off with some of his men seeing a galley he was having built over at the town nearby, and would be back soon. Then she brought us some claret and food while we men settled ourselves down to wait for him to return.

Mariota spoke with her longer, and the two were soon in deep conversation about people and places I knew little of, and cared less for, if the truth was known of it. Mary returned to her weaving, and Mariota helped her while she worked by winding some yarn onto the shuttles for our hostess. I leaned my back against the stone wall, and dozed off.

I must have slept but a few minutes for the scene in the hall was barely changed when I felt someone tugging at the sleeve of my shift.

"Muirteach," whispered Mariota, "Muirteach, wake up."

"What is it then? Are they back yet?"

"No, Muirteach, but he is here."

I was suddenly wide-awake. I looked around, but Mary had left her loom. Mariota continued. "The bard. Mary was telling me of it. He came four nights ago."

I thought. That was not the day he had left Colonsay, claiming to be headed towards Mull.

"Were you telling Mary it is him we are seeking?"

Mariota shook her head. "No, Muirteach. She is gone now, to see to something in the kitchens for a bit."

"Remember, Mariota, he is not knowing we know of him. I can be fabricating some business of my uncle's with Lachlan while we try and find out more information."

"But Muirteach, we have the pin. Does that not prove he murdered Sheena? Why not just take him the now?"

"He will not run. He does not know that we have it. Let us wait awhile, and speak with the MacLean about it all, privately, like, for we may be needing some of his men."

Mariota acquiesced, but I could tell from the set of her mouth that she was not happy about my decision. It was just about then that the MacLean, followed by his tail of retainers, entered the hall. His wife greeted him, and then we came forward to meet him.

Lachlan MacLean was a tall, broad-shouldered man, with not a little of the Norse in his looks, from his blond hair and beard and the angular planes of his face. A well-favored man he was, and I could see why Mary had insisted on her way when she wed him. They made a fine-looking couple together, indeed, standing there together in the new hall.

I scanned the ranks of his retainers. The MacLean's own bard was there, easy to recognize from the small harp slung over his back, but I did not see Seòras. The *gille mor,* the bodyguards, looked to be a strong group of men, and I knew I would feel the better having them with us when the time came to take our man.

I asked to speak with the MacLean in privacy, on the pretext of business from Uncle Gillespic, and when we were settled behind a carved wooden screen in a corner of the hall, I told him of our mission. He nodded.

"Aye, the man is here. But are you sure he is a murderer?"

"We have the proof, at least that he killed the woman." I took the pin out of my pouch and showed it to him.

"Where did you get it?"

I told him the sad story. The MacLean nodded, and something glinted in his eyes.

"It must be him. But I am not wanting to take him here in

this hall, where he has played music for us and eaten my bread and drunk of my wine, for all that he may have murdered the Prior of Oronsay. We will get him outside, Muirteach, and then you shall take him, and you can cart him off to His Lordship and that will be the end of it."

I hoped so.

"Where is he the now?"

"I am not certain. The man has come here before, he is a fine harper, but he has the wanderlust in his feet, and keeps himself to himself. Seòras goes off alone in the days; he rambles in the moors and the forests. I always thought him fey, half-faerie, not one to do murder."

He drained his cup, and shrugged his broad shoulders. "Och well, most men will do murder. I am not knowing why I was not thinking he would do so."

And so we laid our plans while the summer afternoon drew to a close.

The evening came, finally, and the feasting. The torches gave off a piney resinous scent as they flared, set in their iron holders in the stone walls, and a fine smell of food mixed with the smoke in the air. The Seneschal assigned the places, touching each seat with his white wand. There were no nobles to be placated, or argue over precedence, and all sat down agreeably to begin the feast.

I was surprised to find myself at the head table, in fair proximity to the MacLean and his wife, and Mariota, who had been placed next to Mary. Their two heads bent close together, exchanging confidences in that manner women have.

I scanned the assembly to find Seòras. He sat after the Mac-Lean's own bard and harper, at the far end of the table. He did not see me, although no doubt he would recognize me from Donald Dubh's, or Aorig's.

He ate silently, not speaking much, but when the time for

music came, after the MacLean's own harper had entertained us, he played again with that great skill of his, with sounds of fierce, fleeting wildness. Such sadness I heard in it, so that my own hand shook as I drained the wine in my cup, listening.

That night Mariota was to sleep in Lady Mary's bower, with the Lady herself and her serving-women, while I slept in the hall. After the feasting ended, I looked for the chance to speak with her, but did not see her when I scanned the crowd. Instead, I heard the noise of her footstep, and again smelled that elder-flower scent of hers. I turned, and again I felt that funny leap in my heart at the sight of her.

"Ah, Muirteach."

I told her of the plan I had made with the MacLean.

"What if he escapes?"

"How could he be doing that, Mariota? Does the man have a boat? I am thinking, even if he were to have one, we could catch him easily, with the galley."

The set of Mariota's chin made me think she had not been convinced, but she said no more. The torchlight flickered over her features, the oval face, the blue eyes looking darker in the dim light.

"So we will be taking him to Islay?" she asked.

"I am thinking so. For himself was wanting to see to the matter."

"But Muirteach, suppose he did not kill your father? You yourself said so, that he came with you to Colonsay from Finlaggan that day. What if he only used the same method to kill Sheena?"

"And how was he knowing of it?" I returned. "No, Mariota, do not be worrying about it. We are sure he killed Sheena, and for that he deserves punishment. And we must question him about the other affair; he may know something of it or perhaps have done the deed himself. Leave it to the MacLean and I, and we shall have him, and the affair will be ended. Then you can go back to your MacNeill."

I could see her eyes widen in the torchlight.

"You were hearing about that? From who?"

I wished I had not mentioned it. "My cousin on Islay, it was, that told me of it."

"Oh," was all Mariota said, and smiled a little smile. "People talk, but perhaps they are not knowing all of the matter." Just then Lady Mary rose from the hall, preparing to withdraw with her women. Mariota reached out to touch my sleeve.

I yearned to jerk away, even as I savored her sweet touch, for was she not promised to another? But I did not move, and instead stayed still while she spoke, feeling the warmth of her hand where it rested on my arm through the linen of my sleeve.

"I must go now, Muirteach," she said. "I shall be seeing you in the morning, and we will pray things go as you think they will." Then she left the hall, following after Mary and the others.

Seòras sat, with the MacLean's own bard and harper, drinking and eating a bit now that most of the feasting had ended. I walked over and joined them there.

"And so it is Muirteach, is it not?" Seòras said. "The scribe from Colonsay. What is bringing you to Mull?"

"Uncle Gillespic had some business with the MacLean and he was sending me about it," I explained. "But we have finished and I shall be leaving tomorrow."

"Aye. The MacLean was asking me to play for you, when you leave."

"It is a fine hand you have for the music. It would be a privilege indeed to have you play for us as we cast off."

The next morning, early, we prepared to leave. The sun's light was barely changing the darkness to a pearly gray color as we walked down to the pebbly beach in front of the rocky mass that held Duart. The mists looked to be coming in from the mainland, and wrapped the world in shrouds, making it all look like the ghostly underworld of the old stories of the dawn of time.

I swallowed, and my throat caught on the swallow, with a strange dry feel to it. I had gone over the plan with the crew. For all that I had spoken so confidently to Mariota, I wondered if things would go awry, and for sure this mist would not be helping matters if they did.

Mariota stood where the jetty touched the shore, almost hidden by the fog, speaking with Lady Mary, while the MacLean and some of his men who had come down to see us off encircled the group. Seòras, at the MacLean's asking, played on his harp while the Colonsay men prepared the boat to depart.

I nodded and two brawny men of the crew came to stand by him, one on each side of him, yet still he continued to play, finishing the air. As his fingers fell away from the harp, they grabbed his hands and held them behind his back, and the harp fell to the stones of the beach. I heard the sharp sound of splintering wood and saw it lying there, broken.

"What is the meaning of this?" he asked, but I thought he knew even as he spoke.

"Seòras," I replied, "are you remembering the woman Sheena that was killed on Colonsay? We have found her murderer."

"What is that to me?"

I drew the pin from my cloak. "Are you not knowing this brooch?" I asked, holding it up before him. A shaft of sunlight somehow found its way through the mist and glinted on the silver of it for a moment, before the clouds covered the sun again.

I watched him go pale underneath the weathered tan of his face. "How came you by that?" he asked.

"It was found on your own mother's body. On Islay. For she

is dead, Seòras, she killed herself. But before that deed was done, this pin belonged to Sheena. I saw her wear it, often enough. And by that I am knowing that it was you who killed her, and later gave the pin to your own dam."

He laughed, with that same wildness in it I had heard in his harping. "Och, so you think you have solved it all as easy as that—" he cried. "It is little enough you are knowing of it all, Muirteach."

His words sent a chill down the spine of me, for were they not the exact same words that Sheena had said to me, that first day, when I had gone to speak with her about my father's death?

And then the harper turned into a wild thing, and twisted away from the men in the mist. They tried to restrain him but could not, such was the mad strength he possessed. He fought like the shape-shifter, and got free of them, and then, to my great sorrow, he lunged forward, and there was no man there to stop him. His hand reached out, faster than an adder, and grabbed Mariota, dragging her with him, atop the rock that served as the jetty below the castle.

I saw the flash of steel and his dagger at her throat.

"You will not be coming any closer," he said.

I watched Mariota's eyes wide above his hand that covered her mouth, and as she twisted to get free he pricked her white neck with the dagger point, and the red blood dripped down on the fairness of her skin.

Mariota grew still, and he let go of her mouth and held her arms behind her with his other hand, still keeping the knife to her throat. She stood quiet now, and did not struggle against him.

"You have seen that I will do what I say," he cried, walking backwards down the jetty, all the while holding her before him like a shield. "So now we will just be getting into this fine boat here, and if any of you are following us, she will die. For if I am to die as a murderer, what matters one murder more?"

He laughed again, that same horrible laugh, and pushed Mariota into a small boat tied at the end of the rough jetty. I heard the thud of her hitting the wood of the boat and tried to run forward, but Seòras, who had jumped in after her, grabbed Mariota up and held her before him, taking the knife and touching it to her neck in a warning. Her eyes were closed, and she hung senseless in his arms.

"No closer, Muirteach," he said. "Or she will die." And I knew he meant the words he spoke.

Then he let her fall back down into the boat while he hoisted the sail of the *curragh*. An archer could have taken him then, but to my sorrow and despair not one among the MacLean's men, nor mine, had their bows ready that early morning, although swords and dirks we had in plenty.

"No, Muirteach," cautioned the MacLean in a low voice to me, "for we shall find him. He cannot get far in that small boat, and we shall overtake him."

"And then he will kill Mariota," said Lady Mary. "There is no following him, Lachlan, or her death will be on your head."

And so the sail was hoisted, and caught in the breeze that even then blew through the mist, and the small boat left the harbor and disappeared into the sea.

CHAPTER 20

"I know where he will take her," I said, the knowledge of it bitter as oak gall within me, and I told the MacLean about the small boat I had seen on Nave Island. "That is where he will go to ground, I am sure of it."

"At least that is the place to start. And won't you be telling her father of this, as well? His Lordship himself will no doubt send men to find them. They can scour Islay for them."

"If he has not taken her some other place." My certainty of a moment before had fled, and I felt only horror, mixed with self-recrimination and shame that the matter had gone so terribly awry. For Mariota's safety had been my trust, and I had failed her, as I had failed Sheena before, blinded as I was by my own overconfidence and faulty logic.

"I will send a messenger to Finlaggan," said the MacLean.

"And we shall follow after them. With a crew of twelve perhaps we shall overtake them, if he is not recognizing our boat."

We went then, the MacLean and I, into the village of Craignure. No one had seen the small boat pass that way, and it appeared they had not gone to ground in Mull. The MacLean commandeered a boat from one of the merchants there, that Seòras would be less like to recognize, and said he would send word to Finlaggan with my uncle's more recognizable galley and that crew. So later that morning I found myself again sailing for Nave Island, trying to ignore the sick dread that griped at my bowels.

Suppose he killed Mariota? And wasn't it I, with my foolish pride and false certainty, that had put her in danger?

I cursed the wind for not blowing faster, and cursed my leg, and physical weakness, that had prevented me from tackling the man as he had stood there, his knife against that beautiful throat, and cursed my own lack of wisdom for putting her in danger at all, at all.

I should have sent her packing back to Islay from Colonsay, where she would have been safe, for all that she had not wanted to return. And what would her father be saying to me about it all, how could I tell him what had happened to his beautiful and much-loved daughter?

Just north of the Garvellachs we saw a sail ahead, and proceeded cautiously, thinking it might be Seòras, but the sail proved to be just a fishing boat. We hailed them, and found that they had indeed seen the small boat earlier. But it had not gone south towards Colonsay and Islay. They had seen it turn east, between Luing and Lunga, towards Scarba and the Strait of Corryvreckan.

"*Dia*," muttered the captain of my boat, "he'd never be trying to take such a small ship through her. Not alone, with no crew."

"Perhaps he does not mean to," another of the crew suggested. "He could just be heading for the mainland by going this way."

I did not think so, remembering the man's fey laughter, as he held the knife to Mariota's throat.

"It is not a bad tide," the captain said, thinking out loud. "Perhaps they will make it through the Cailleach."

The Cailleach, they call her, the old hag, the whirlpool that, it is said, killed Prince Brecan of Norway so many years ago. He dared to anchor his boat for three days and three nights in the whirlpool, and all for love it was, to win the hand of the princess of the island.

He brought three ropes with him to anchor the boat, one of hemp, one of wool, and one of maiden's hair. But the last rope did not hold, for one of the women was not virgin, and the brave prince drowned, his body dragged down to the bottom of the sea, to be the old hag's bridegroom.

"On a fair day, with the wind from the southeast, or from the north, one can make it through, with luck," the captain was saying. "But one must know the strait. What of that man?"

"I am thinking he is a good sailor," I said, remembering the boat on Nave Island, the same small boat he sailed in now. Good enough to sail to Colonsay and back to Islay, without being noticed. "I am thinking he knows the waters in these parts."

"As do I, myself," returned the captain. "Well, we shall follow them through, then."

And he turned the boat through the narrow passage between Luing, on our left, and the grassy hill that was Lunga to our right. I heard a dull roaring sound and asked the captain about it.

"That will be the Cailleach, making her howl," he answered.

At the south end of Lunga the water poured and churned in a narrow passage. "The *Bealach a' Choin Ghlais,* the gray dogs," said the captain. "If you have the nerve, they are a short passage to the Garvellachs from here."

We passed them by on our right, those growling dogs that poured out in a torrent from Lunga, and followed the coast of Scarba on our right until the tip of Jura appeared, and the strait of the old hag between the two islands. The noise of the roaring grew louder in my ears.

"I am thinking," I said, "that he means to take the boat in through the Cailleach, and perhaps anchor along the coast, thinking that no one will be looking for him there. On Jura he can hide well enough, there are not so many people on the western side of the island."

"Aye," agreed the captain, as he turned our boat into the strait. "Say a prayer, if you've a mind to. For we shall be needing the help of God and his Saints to get through this. The tide is turning, and the wind looks to be shifting. Here, we will be needing everyone to row."

As I positioned myself at an oar, I heard him mutter a prayer as he pulled on the rudder.

Power of surf be thine, power of swell be thine, power of the sap
of my reason.
Thou shalt journey upward and come again down,
thou shalt journey over ocean and come again hither.

I crossed myself, and murmured a prayer to Saint Christopher for his protection, for it looked as though we would have need of it.

I set to rowing against the current. Of a sudden I saw ahead, where the gulf narrowed, a ragged line of white breakers, and felt the spray on my face as the boat began to pitch, turning this way and that despite what direction the captain held the rudder. We tore off course, and the rocks of Scarba raced by, now starboard, now port, now astern, as we circled, caught in the relentless grasp of the Cailleach.

"Look," shouted the captain, and to the right the surface of the sea seemed suddenly greasy, as though a puddle of melted tallow had been poured on the top of the surging waves. As I gazed, mesmerized, at the flatness, a plume of water spurted upwards, fell back on itself, and swirled, forming a perfect vortex, a descent, so it seemed to me, into the mouth of a watery Hell.

"*Pull!*" shouted the captain and we bent all our strength to the oars, edging imperceptibly away from the whirlpool, only to find another flat circle appearing to our left.

We changed course, pulling this way and that amongst the maws of the old hag, time and time again escaping one vortex only to see another whirlpool opening before us. My muscles ached, and I could not say how long we were in the jaws of the Cailleach. Time seemed to have no meaning, except that every breath, every pull on the oars, straining against the grip of the hag, seemed an eternity. Exhausted, I thought I could pull no more, but still I strove on the oars, until before me I saw a wall of green sea, fully as high as the mast of our ship it was. This is the end, I thought, but we climbed through that barrier of the ocean, and burst out, suddenly, onto the open waters.

Such heavenly quiet and stillness were there, after the hell we had survived. The sun poured down on our drenched and salt-soaked bodies and the black rocks of the islands, and gulls swooped over the calmness of the open sea.

"We were not her victims today," said the captain, with some satisfaction, "but I am thinking she has not gone hungry, after all. Look there—"

And with a sinking heart I followed his pointing and saw, on the rocks of the coast of Jura, splinters of wood and a mast, a tangled sail washed up on shore, and what looked to be the remains of a small boat. But of bodies I saw none.

"The hag has claimed them," said the captain. Indeed it seemed to be so. We had beached the boat, and searched the shore near the wreck. We saw no footprints, although, I told myself desperately that the rocky ground might not have held the mark. But a search of the countryside yielded nothing, except a few wild goats, contentedly grazing amongst the rocks, and they did not speak of what they had seen that day. The captain must have told the truth. They had drowned.

I thought of the cold waters closing over Mariota, and steal-
ing the breath away out of her body, and shuddered. I hoped
she had gone quickly, not struggling in the grip of the Cailleach, but I feared that that had not been the way it had happened.

The sun was low in the sky, and the crew sodden and salt-
soaked, exhausted, but I continued to search until the sky grew
dark. And all the time I searched I wept for Mariota. My tears
wet the beach, mingling with the cold gray waters of the Cailleach.

*I must report to His Lordship at Finlaggan, and somehow find the
words to tell the Beaton about his daughter. And that would be setting all the Beatons, and the MacNeills as well, against me,* I
thought, exhausted, but even that did not matter. Perhaps I
would let Mariota's fine betrothed kill me, when he caught up
with me, and that would be the end of it all.

But the murderer of my father had been found. For all that it
made no sense to me, he must have crossed to Colonsay and
killed my father, out of jealousy over Sheena I supposed, but
then been forced to kill her himself when she had seen the
murder. And the harp pin that little Sean had showed to me; he
had not received it that night the Seòras had played for us at
Aorig's. He must have gotten it at his mother's house. Perhaps
the harper had given it to him, or he had found it after the man
had left.

A fire had been kindled, and shelter for the night found in a
cave facing the western sea. Someone had caught a rabbit, but
the good smell of the roasting meat did not tempt me to eat.

On impulse I took the quartz stone from my pouch and rolled
it between my fingers, looking at the firelight reflected in its
depths. As if, I thought bitterly, like some seer I would see
Mariota in it. But I am no such seer.

The stone remained dull and opaque and at length I replaced the crystal in my pouch. Then I sat unmoving, staring into the flames until they died to white ashes, and the last of the firelight faded to black, then merged with the greater darkness of the sky. Only then did I lie down on the hard and rocky ground, but I did not sleep.

I reached Finlaggan late the next day. The captain from Mull took me as far as the port at Bunahabhain, but not before we made another detour, at my request, to that fisherman's hut on Nave Island.

We found no nets or other gear there, but a few provisions. It looked to be a hiding place of some sort, and I realized that from that spot Seòras could easily have taken his small boat to the Strand and killed my father. He then could have returned to Islay in time to be playing the harp at Finlaggan when I myself had arrived. We had taken him back to Colonsay that next day, where he had stayed until he murdered Sheena.

But when we stopped at Padraic's hut we did not find him there alive. He lay dead on his bed, strangled.

The captain finally beached the boat in Bunahabhain, and then left for Mull, with the promise of a fine reward from His Lordship along with most of the money I had in my purse.

I kept enough to pay for a horse, and took the road to Finlaggan. It was not too long before I saw the causeway leading to the manor house on the large island glinting in the evening sun. The Lord of the Isles, I was told, had gone to Dunyvaig, to see to some new galleys that were being built there, but he was expected back that same evening. And so I waited, cooling my heels, and, coward that I was, praying I would not see Fearchar and have to tell him about the death of his daughter.

I discovered that the messenger from Mull had arrived the day before, with the news of the stolen boat and the capture of

Mariota, but His Lordship, along with the Beaton, had already left for Dunyvaig when the messenger arrived. And the messenger, owing his greater allegiance to the MacLean, had not waited to deliver his message personally to His Lordship but had simply given it to the steward there and then returned to Mull, which meant neither His Lordship nor the Beaton were knowing of what had transpired.

I wondered if Fearchar even knew his daughter had left Islay for Colonsay at all. Perhaps even now, he believed her safe at Balinaby.

So I mused on such unhappy thoughts while I waited, drinking claret, and then more claret, trying to erase from my mind's eye the image of the tortured look in Mariota's eyes as Seòras had held the knife to her throat. But in this I was not successful.

That night a messenger arrived with the news that himself had been detained at Dunyvaig, and would not be returning for several more days at the latest, as the galleys he was having built had some difficulties and he was reluctant to leave until the problem was solved.

I decided to go seek him, reasoning he would be happy to hear of the solving of the murder of my father, as that would mean the Holy Father would be off his back and his political dilemma solved neatly. As to how the Beaton would react to the news of his daughter's loss I dared not think.

And so the next morning, after the messenger had rested, I returned with the messenger to Dunyvaig. The man spoke but little, which suited my mind this day. The sky glimmered a clear blue above us as we rode through the grassy hills. I would have enjoyed the riding and the good gray horse beneath my legs, had it not been for the sore weight of my heart in my chest.

At length we reached Dunyvaig Castle. It sits on the rocks, looking out towards Kintyre to the east and Antrim to the south.

A fine imposing castle it is, with the large curtain wall and the grand outer courtyard, leading to the small inner yard, sitting high atop the rocks overlooking the sea. Several galleys anchored in the Lagavulin Bay in front of the castle, and there was much activity, with sailors working on repairs and seeing to the ships.

We entered through the gate into the outer yard. Here also men hurried, several smiths worked on armor at some forges, while in another corner cows and cattle milled. A young boy hurried to the kitchens with a basket of eggs and two squawking chickens under his arm. The messenger and I gave our horses to a lad from the stables, and I followed the man into the keep, and up some narrow stairs to the great hall of the castle.

An imposing place it looked, with a richly painted ceiling, and walls hung with tapestry. At the end of the hall I spied the Lord of the Isles, deep in conversation with a number of his bodyguard and another man, dressed in work clothes.

As we neared I overheard their discussion, something about numbers of oars and I guessed that they spoke of the new galleys and that this man was the master boatbuilder. Around the hall lounged other of His Lordship's retainers. A harper played idly, although no one, not even the great staghounds lounging by the fire, paid much attention to the music. I looked for the Beaton, and, shamefully, felt relief when I did not see him in the room.

His Lordship looked up, glimpsed us, and finished conferring with the shipwright. He sat down in the high chair sitting at the end of the hall, then beckoned us forward, and we approached.

"So it is Muirteach, finally," he said, drinking from the silver *mether* which sat by his side on a small, richly carved, wooden table. "And have you been solving the murder for me yet?"

"Indeed I have," I answered with far more bravado than I was feeling. "But we have found another person slain. And the murderer himself is now dead, as well, drowned in the Cailleach some two days ago."

"Whoever was he, then?"

"It was Seòras, the harper."

I heard a murmur of surprise from those men milling in the hall. I told them of Father Padraic's murder. "I am thinking he kept a small boat on Nave Island, and from there he was traveling to Colonsay to kill the Prior."

"That priest was from the Rhinns. And he had kin there," interjected one of His Lordship's retainers.

And Padraic, out of his kind heart, had let his sister's boy use the hut from time to time, I realized, the "poor soul" the priest had mentioned to me. Now he had joined his sister, Alsoon, in death.

His Lordship was not looking convinced. "And what reason would he be having to do all of that?" he asked, sipping from his silver glass.

"Jealousy over a woman. The woman Sheena, my father's handfasted wife, whom he also murdered. I am thinking because she knew of the first murder. And then perhaps Padraic came to know of it, and so he was killed as well." I remembered the look on Seòras's face as he held the knife to Mariota. "The man was crazed."

His Lordship considered a moment, then his face broke into a smile. "So it was not one of the canons. That is very good, Muirteach, very good indeed. I am well pleased with your solution."

I noticed he did not say whether or not he believed me, and I found that rankled a bit, for all that I knew I spoke the truth.

"Now, are you wanting some drink?"

A retainer quickly brought some ale. It tasted good in the heat of the day, and I gulped some of it down, out of nervousness.

"There is something else, Your Lordship," I said, after I had finished the ale. "Some news which I am doubting you will be liking so well. And I am knowing that others here will like it even less."

"And what would that be?"

I told him of Mariota's being taken hostage by Seòras, and her death, along with his own, in the Cailleach.

"A great pity that is indeed," observed His Lordship, hardly seeming affected by the news. "And an unwise woman she was, as well, to go running off to Colonsay as she did."

"Your Lordship," I protested, "she was a great help to me in solving the murders. Were it not for her bringing me this pin," and I drew it from my pouch to show him, "we would not have known for sure that it was Seòras who committed the crime."

"Her father will not be happy to hear of the news, when you are telling him, Muirteach," responded His Lordship. "And the MacNeill she was to marry as well."

The orator leaned forward and whispered something in the ear of the Lord of the Isles. The Lord paused, took another drink of his wine, and then added, "Oh, MacMhurich here is telling me that the betrothal was broken off. Recently, and by the woman herself. Now why, are you thinking, would she be doing such a thing?"

"I do not know, sir. Nor, am I thinking, does it matter much the now."

"Well, you are no doubt right in that, Muirteach. But you will be having a sad thing to do, when the Beaton is returning from his doctoring. For I leave the telling of it to you, since it was your poor judgment that led her to this sad end."

And he turned to speak with another of his retainers, and I surmised my interview was at an end. Miserable and bitter, I bowed to him, wanting nothing more than to crawl away, like some injured hound, to lick my wounds, or perhaps to try and drink myself to sick forgetfulness. Yet I sensed even there I would find no solace.

"Oh, and Muirteach," he added, as I prepared to leave the hall, "just you be seeing my steward, there, and be writing a letter for me to the King, and one to the Holy Father in Rome, telling them of the solution to the murder. And then we will see about a reward for your labor on this matter."

"None is necessary, sir. The man murdered my father."

"Yes, but you will be wanting an honor-price. Or if you are not wanting it, the Priory should have one, I am thinking. Well, away with you, and be writing the letters the now. Then this matter will be ended, and good riddance to it."

The steward led me to a small anteroom and brought writing supplies. I composed my letters by the light of the sun, shining through the tiny slit window in the wall, and wondered how I would tell Fearchar of his daughter's death.

I had just about finished when I heard a commotion from the hall. I stood up from my writing bench and stepped to the doorway to listen. A disheveled messenger stood before His Lordship. The man, obviously frightened, panted, and looked as though he had run a far ways.

"What is it?" demanded the steward. "What is this news that brings you here so suddenly?"

"A madman—" gasped the man. "A madman has killed the priest of the chapel at Port Asabuis, and now he has claimed sanctuary in that same chapel!"

CHAPTER 21

"Tell us of it," demanded His Lordship, listening intently as the man repeated his story.

"What does this man look like?" I interrupted. "And how did he get to the Oa?"

I did not dare hope, and yet, how many such madmen could there be on one island?

"I do not know," responded the man. "We were out working the fields, and heard a hubbub from the chapel, and then the women came running through the corn, saying that there was murder done. And the priest lay there, in front of the chapel he was, with his hand outstretched, just touching the cross, and blood all over the walk—"

"And so you were coming here?"

The man nodded, awed by his surroundings.

"When did all this happen?"

"This morning it was. I took a boat and came here, for it was known you were here at Dunyvaig. You must be helping us, Your Lordship," cried the man. "It is the devil himself has got into our church."

"I am thinking it is no devil," said His Lordship, "but a man, although perhaps he is indeed a devil if the Cailleach herself is spitting him out. Well, let us be sending some men there to be seeing about it all, then."

"You must let me go," I demanded of His Lordship.

"Aye, Muirteach, I am thinking that I must."

And so it was that a short while later a good galley, filled with sixteen strong men, along with the messenger and myself, set sail from Lagavulin Bay and crossed the short distance to the Oa Peninsula. We beached the boat along a short stretch of sandy beach, ringed on either side by high granite cliffs, and climbed the narrow path leading up the steep rocks to the chapel, dedicated to Saint Ailbhe, one of the boatmen had told me. At a distance things looked peaceful enough, but as we neared the site we saw a dark stain on the flagstones in the front of the church, before the great stone cross, and a cluster of men surrounding the chapel.

"He has claimed sanctuary," one of the local men told us as we drew closer. "He is inside."

"Was he alone?"

The man shook his head. "I am not knowing that. I was not here when it happened. Here," he said, gesturing to the dark pool of blood which still lay on the stones, "is where he was killing the priest."

"What led to this? Why did he kill the priest? Did the priest try to stop him?"

"Och, no. The priest was outside here, he had just finished the morning Mass and had stepped outside, and everyone else had left. And then, I am thinking that the madman had hidden himself, somehow, behind the rock there, and came after the priest, demanding sanctuary. But perhaps the priest was not being fast enough with his answer, for it is said the madman took out his *sgian dubh* and cut him, and the man bled to death while the lunatic took shelter in the church."

"And so you are thinking he was alone."

"No one was here to see it happen. We just found the priest here, when Rhodri came to bring him some eggs."

"So then how are you knowing he is inside?"

"Look." The man pointed to the trail of bloodied footprints

leading to inside the chapel. But there was only one set of prints, not two, although there was a smear of blood as if something had been dragged inside with him.

The men from Dunyvaig milled around, while I thought about what to do. There was much discussion, with some of them all for rushing into the church and extirpating the devil, while others crossed themselves, unwilling to breach sanctuary and whatever demon had claimed it.

"Wait here," I finally spoke, "and I will go into the church and see who is there. I am thinking it is Seòras himself, the harper, and if so it is no demon, nor devil, but a man only."

The men stood back to let me enter the church. I tried to walk confidently, despite my limp. I went unarmed and entered the chapel.

"Seòras," I cried into the darkness. "Is it you, then?"

The man stood, and indeed it was Seòras, returned from the dead.

"We were thinking the Cailleach had had you."

He spoke, finally. "Aye, I saw you there, looking for me, and not finding me. And I watched as you sailed away, leaving me there, snug in my tiny cave high up in the rocks of the hills."

"And how were you getting here from Jura?" I asked, approaching a little closer in the dim light of the chapel.

"Walked along the coast until I was finding a small boat. And then I took it, and left the hunters there on Jura, and sailed here to Islay. I thought of this small chapel, and needed a place of sanctuary." He laughed, and the sound of it chilled me to the marrow.

"And what of Mariota?"

"And wouldn't you just be wanting to know?" He laughed. "Well, I will tell you, after all. She is here, with me, the now."

"Let me see her."

He gestured to what looked like a bundle of rags lying against the wall of the chapel, near the altar. I saw that the bundle was tied by a rope to his wrist.

"Is she alive?"

"Aye, she is. She is mine, Muirteach, for it was I that saved her from the Cailleach."

"Mariota!" I called. "Mariota, it is Muirteach here. Can you hear me?"

The bundle stirred, and the ice that had frozen around my heart seemed to melt a little as I watched the bundle move.

Mariota sat up. "Muirteach," she said, and I felt the ice crack apart and my heart spring back to life like the stream does when the ice melts in the spring.

Seòras jerked roughly on the rope, pulling Mariota to her feet, and then dragged her towards him and held her up for me to see. "You must not be speaking with him, mind, for you are mine the now. Are you not, Mariota?"

Mariota nodded, a small, tight, motion, but I saw her eyes glance towards me.

"Do not be worrying, Mariota," I told her. "We shall be getting you out of here." And I prayed that I was not lying to her as I said the words.

"Do not try and speak with her again," Seòras cautioned, tightening his grip on Mariota, "for I still have my knife, and will use it on her."

"Give yourself up, Seòras," I said. "For we have sixteen men outside and you will not prevail against us."

"Ah, but I have Mariota, and my sharp knife as well."

"You cannot win against us."

"I have claimed sanctuary," cried Seòras, "and none can gainsay that."

"You gainsaid my father, as he claimed sanctuary."

"He did not reach sanctuary, Muirteach, and he was deserving of none. So God punished him."

"He was not punished by God, Seòras, but he was killed by man. As you, of all people should know. But I am not understanding the why of it. All that, over Sheena. Was she worth it, then, Seòras?"

Seòras laughed then, a wild laugh with the music of his harp in it. The sound of it echoed off the stone of the chapel, bouncing back and forth again over the rock walls until the last note of it died away. "Is that what you are thinking of it, Muirteach? Well enough, that is."

"And then you killed Sheena, because she saw the first murder."

He nodded.

"And then you killed Father Padraic, there on the island, and your mother killed herself."

"I was not giving her much of a choice in it, after she heard what I told her."

"About the murders?"

"That, and other things I had to say to her. She took the pin and opened her veins with that great sharp point of it, and I watched her as she did it."

"Your own mother."

"Aye."

Seòras suddenly pulled Mariota closer to him. "Now away with you, Muirteach." I saw his dagger blade flash as he held it out, close to her. "It is tired I am of speaking with you. And you cannot be touching me here, for I have claimed sanctuary," he taunted. "Away with you."

I grew cold with the fear that he would use that bright blade against Mariota, and so I did as he asked me to. The light outside blinded me after the cool dimness of the chapel, but the sun did little to warm me and I shivered in the brightness of the light.

I spoke with the men, and we made our plan. We asked the

villagers for green wood, wood that would not burn, but would smoke, and built fires in the front threshold of the church. We would smoke them out of their sanctuary, like foxes from their den.

And what if Seòras did not emerge? If that was the case, I told myself we would break into the chapel from the rear window, behind the altar, and in the smoke and confusion I swore I would free Mariota and let her captor burn to death in this Hell of his own making.

The wood was brought and the fires were kindled. The thick smoke filled the air while we waited. Some of the sixteen men from Dunyvaig surrounded the doorway to the chapel, while others waited in the back, near the narrow windows behind the altar, and threw more burning brands through the narrow windows. The breeze blew from the sea, and drove the smoke back into the dark interior of the church. We waited, while the sun sank lower over the western sea, a red ball through the haze of our smoke.

There came a noise, and the harper emerged from the doorway, looking like one of the demons from Hell, with the black smoke and the flickering light of the flames from inside the church surrounding him. The fire had caught on some of the altar cloths and the wooden rood screen within the chapel, and burned more strongly with each passing moment.

He held a burning brand before him as he came out of the church and pulled Mariota after him, still tied to him with the rope around her neck. She retched and coughed from the smoke.

Seòras, too, coughed, but his eyes gleamed white in the smoke-smeared skin of his face, like a bright flash of lightning in the black storm of a sky, or like the flash of the blade of the dagger he still held against Mariota's throat.

"You must let her go," I said, trying to reason with him. "We are many against you. You cannot be winning."

"Ah, but I can be using your own weapons against you," he said, holding the burning torch before him like a sword and brandishing it into the faces of those men who tried to approach him.

Seòras edged closer to the edge of the circle, then struck like a viper with his knife, darting through the ring of men, and a cry rang out. One of our men lay on the ground, with blood staining his tunic.

"Where did they run?"

The man pointed in the direction of the high cliffs, behind the chapel. I looked in the direction he pointed, and could just make out through the smoky dusk Seòras, dragging Mariota behind him. She fell to her knees, and I feared she would strangle as he jerked on the rope to pull her up again, before he reached the cliff and turned to face us.

I gestured to the others to stand back, but I myself walked closer to them.

"Not so close now, Muirteach," he said. "Or she will be going over the edge. Will you not, *mo chridhe?*"

Mariota's face looked a ghostly white blur in the dimness but she looked at me and nodded. "He will do it, Muirteach," she whispered, her voice hoarse and cracked from the smoke and the fire. "You must be believing him."

"I told you not to be speaking to him," said Seòras, taking a step backwards, towards the edge of the cliff. The sound of the surf battering the rocks below pounded in my ears, and I had to raise my voice as I answered him.

"Seòras," I asked, "what is the profit in this? You cannot win. We know you have done murder, but why? Surely the woman Sheena was not worth all this suffering."

"Aye, you were saying something of the sort, back there, were you not Muirteach? You are mistaken if you are thinking that is why I killed your father."

"Was it not for Sheena? She was your lover, was she not?"

"Indeed, and she was, but I would not kill your father over her. Whyever should I, since I was already tupping his own mistress, and him none the wiser for it. No, now, that was not the way of it at all, Muirteach."

"Then why?" I saw that his hold on the rope had lessened, just a little, and felt a faint glimmering of hope. "Why, Seòras? For I confess I am not understanding this."

"For what he did to me. When I was at the Priory."

"But you were just a young boy."

"Indeed, Muirteach, and were you thinking that women were the only thing your father lusted after? I am surprised he was not buggering you, for all that you were his own son. But he liked well-favored boys, and you were not so well-favored as all that, were you? Not with your shriveled leg, and your limping, and your sniveling. He always liked my voice, like an angel's he said it was. He used to have me sing for him, after."

His face contorted in a grimace, and I saw the wetness of tears on his cheeks. But I also saw he had dropped his hold on the rope. And from the change in Mariota's expression, I knew that she had felt that slackness. I stepped closer, hoping to keep him speaking, and Seòras, intent on his own emotion, did not notice at first.

"And it was for that you killed him," I said, as Mariota shifted her weight a little, edging away from him.

"Aye, indeed. For that. I was leaving Sheena's that night. I would sail from the Nave Island to Colonsay, to visit her from time to time. I had known her since she was a girl. And we had your own father in common, for he used her poorly, as he had her brother, Columbanus, before her. And that is when I saw him, coming to her on the path in the moonlight. He had already crossed the Strand, and the light glimmered on his footsteps in the sand. They looked like molten silver there.

"I had not seen him in years, since I had left the Priory, but he still had that look to him, like a satyr or some lustful demon. And Sheena had been saying that she did not like it that he liked little Sean so, she would see him, fingering the boy's hair, and him his very own son. But that was not why I was killing him."

"And why did you, then?"

"I saw him, there, and he came towards me in the dark, and it was as though I was a child again. I stopped to speak with him, for he did not know who I was, I am thinking. After he had used me in that way as a child, he did not even recognize me, the now. And I remembering it, every day of my life."

"And so you killed him."

"Yes. I waited, and when he returned I spoke with him again. I took down my harp, and said I would play for him, but took a string from it, and sat down close to him, and played, the same song he had had me sing all those times so many years ago."

"And so then he knew you."

"Yes. He knew me at the last. I said to him, 'It is the last music your ears shall hear,' and I took the string out and made to put it around his neck, but he ran from me, coward that he was, across the Strand back towards his Priory. He tried to claim sanctuary, and nearly reached the great cross standing there. But there was no sanctuary for him, just as there had been none for me there so long ago.

"I took a rock, and threw it at him, and brought him down. I strangled him there with my harp string and stuffed his mouth with sand, to choke him even more. And then I took the rock, and pounded him with it as he lay there, until he did not move again. He died with his hand touching the cross."

"And Sheena saw you."

"Aye. She saw, and so she had to die as well, for all that I did not like the killing of her. She had been kind to me, but he had used her, too. I had to kill her, you see, I had no choice. He had used her, and so I could not let her live. She would have suffered from it, as I have. I had to kill her, to save her from that suffering. I killed her gently, for all that."

"Gently enough," I said, horrified at his words.

"She was not expecting it, nor did she suffer overmuch. But it had to be done."

"What of Padraic, on the island?"

"My uncle. Oh, it was your sharp eyes that killed him, Muirteach. He told me of your visit. I feared what you might have told him."

"And Alsoon? Your own mother?"

"Och, she spoke of you as well. And I told her, finally, after all these years, why it was that I ran away from the Priory those fifteen years ago, of what had happened to me there. And of what I had done to your father, and to her own brother, and to Sheena. She had wanted her son to be a priest," he added. "After I ran away, I was not that welcome at her home, I am thinking. But she did not know the why of it all, not until that last day."

"And so she killed herself, when you finally told her of it. And you did not stop her from it."

"No, I did not. She had not saved me, why should I be stopping her? I watched her as she opened her veins, with that sharp silver pin. A fine lot of blood she had in her, my mother. But I took her arms and laid her out nicely, with the brooch on her chest, before I left her lying there and went on to Mull, where you were finding me."

I shuddered, and noticed that Mariota had moved even farther away from him, away from the edge of the cliff. And I saw that some of the men from Dunyvaig had come closer, listening to the tale. I jerked my chin to them, as Seòras came out of his reverie and went to take the rope in his hand again.

But Mariota had picked up the end of it first.

"Mariota, run—" I cried, fearing she would not move quickly enough, but she darted away from him before he could get his hands on the rope. I ran towards him, but he took another step backwards, laughing with that wild laughter. He took yet another step, over the edge, and vanished, and then my eyes saw only empty air before them, and my ears heard only the pounding of the waves against the black rocks.

CHAPTER 22

"Sodomy!"

The Shepherd of the Isles was in a fine temper the next day, after I had told him of it all. He paced in his inner chamber, at Dunyvaig, and I stood by, awkwardly, watching. I had asked to see him alone, to tell him of what had happened. Although with so many of the local folk watching, most of the events of that night were known. Yet Seòras's last confession had not been heard by most of the people there, and it seemed, from what I heard him say now, that His Lordship would insure it remained secret.

"The damned Priory full of sodomites! Your father as well. And that was the motive for it all—"

I nodded.

"Well, at least he is gone, the now."

I was not sure if His Lordship meant my father or Seòras.

"Now, Muirteach," he considered, stopping his pacing and sitting down in a richly carved chair, "I will be needing you to write again both to the King and to his Holy Father. But I do not think you will need to be mentioning all of that to them. Just be telling them we found the murderer, and he took his own life, from the guilt of his misdeeds, perhaps, but that he confessed before he did so. Yes, that will do nicely, I am thinking."

He drank deeply from a goblet that sat on the table nearby, then paused, putting his drink down. His favorite hound looked up at his master a moment, then put his large grizzled head down and went back to sleep.

"Now that is a fine thing indeed, Muirteach," His Lordship continued, after another drink. "There need be no trial, and the story need not come out. And no honor-price to pay, either. For you cannot be demanding restitution from the dead." He smiled, displaying even, wolf-like teeth, and stood up.

"So sit you down, then, and write the letters for me."

He turned and left the withdrawing room for the great hall, followed by his dog, as I seated myself at the table with parchment before me and took up the quill.

I could have predicted that His Lordship would wish the true motive for my father's killing to remain secret. It was not the kind of scandal so cagey a politician as His Lordship would want the King or the Holy Father to know of.

Although the knowledge of that irked me, it seemed the shocking knowledge of my father's worst misdeeds had not hardened my heart. Paradoxically, the horror of that last evening on the Oa seemed to have softened it. Seeing the suffering that Seòras's crazed revenge had left in its wake had cured me of my own bitterness, and the hatred and anger I had so long felt towards my father had evaporated, like mist when the sun burns through it.

You cannot demand restitution from the dead. I thought over His Lordship's words. His Lordship, of course, had been speaking of the honor-price, of cattle and gold. Yet, in another sense I felt my father somehow had made restitution, at least to me.

I had dreamed of him again, that night after Seòras had leaped to his death. My father sat sorrowful, chained in stone. Immobile he rested, imprisoned in his strange rocky dungeon, in the deep, cold heart of the earth, as it seemed to me in the vision. He raised his hand to me, and quoted again from the bard, and then he smiled at me despite his chains. I felt myself smile back at him, in my dream, until he wavered, like smoke from a fire, and vanished.

The crystal I had found by me, after that first vision, I planned to have mounted in silver, to wear as a charm. I hoped I would find it in me to remember the giver of it with kindness, and to forgive all the suffering he had left in his wake, and the hurt he had done to so many, even to Seòras, who had lashed out and killed him in return.

I finished the letters and put them aside in a casket for His Lordship to sign, then entered the hall. A harper stood singing a song about a deerhound and the heroes of the past. I told His Lordship what I had written, and he counted himself pleased with it. And so I joined the feast, in progress already.

"Here," said the Seneschal, pointing with his staff to a seat between the Beaton and his daughter. "Your place is here, this evening."

I sat down, feeling suddenly shy. Mariota looked a bit the worse for her ordeal. Her eyes had a shadowed look to them that I longed to ease, but I fancied they brightened and relaxed when she saw me. She was dressed in a fine blue gown that brought out the color of her eyes, while the high neck of it hid the bruises on her throat. Her hair fell loose down her back like a river of white gold. Her father stood and embraced me, before we all sat down again at the feast.

"And so you have returned my treasure to me," Fearchar said. "I must be thanking you for it. And," he added, looking sidewise at his daughter, "I am thinking she herself will be wanting to thank you in person."

I nodded, in what I hoped was a matter-of-fact way. For what of her betrothal to the MacNeill? Although, from what His Lordship had said yesterday, she had broken it off, it irked me that Mariota herself had not once mentioned it to me. But we did not speak of this, and commenced eating the good venison, frumenty, manchet bread, and fresh cheeses, all washed down with mead and His Lordship's claret. In addition there was salmon, and a fine blancmange, along with numerous other dishes.

Mariota was uncharacteristically silent, and I spoke more with her father. He professed himself curious to hear how the sad affair on the Oa had ended, although, for myself, I could not believe that Mariota had not told him of it.

"She was asleep most of the day, Muirteach. I gave her some poppy juice, and she slept until just a short time ago, when she awoke. There was no stopping her then, but she must change and come down to the feast."

"And why was that?" I asked Mariota, who was delicately reaching for some salmon at the time.

"There was someone I was needing to see," she answered, her eyes downcast.

I looked curiously around the hall, thinking to see her mysterious MacNeill, but I could not be sure who he might be.

"And who was that?" I asked her. "Your MacNeill, then?"

She looked at me, laughed and rolled her eyes a little, like the old Mariota, and it was good to me to see her face lighten and to hear that sound. "Och, no, Muirteach. You were hearing of it from your cousin, were you not?"

I nodded.

"Well, she is not knowing all of it. We were never betrothed, at all. It was just thought we might become so." She blushed, then added, "Or well, we almost were, but I put an end to it."

I felt confused, for that was not exactly what I had heard from His Lordship, when he had spoken of it that day before.

The moment felt awkward, and to avoid further conversation I concentrated on eating my meat tile, nicely spiced as it was. I could swear I heard the Beaton chuckle softly, but then a fit of coughing seized him, so perhaps I was mistaken, as noisy as the hall was with the servants running here and there, bringing more food and drink, and seeing to the feasters.

The meal wound to a close, and the bard began to play. A new song it was, one I had not heard before. At first I did not listen too closely, but suddenly Mariota nudged me with her elbow, hard, and whispered, "Muirteach, it is yourself that they are singing of."

Dogged as the black hound, that does not lose the scent of his prey.
To revenge his own father he followed the crazed one,
Through the wild jaws of the old hag herself, and even onto the precipice.
Where evil found its own swift path to the justice of Our Lord.

"I was not thinking that it was happening quite that way," I muttered to the Beaton, sure that even my ears were crimson. Yet I felt some pride in the song the bard had written, and was glad when Mariota shook her head to disagree.

"It is a fine song, Muirteach, indeed. And close enough it is to the way that things were happening. As I should know."

The song ended, and His Lordship stood to silence the musicians and gain some quiet, which took some time in coming, as the hall was crowded. Then His Lordship spoke.

"You are all knowing of the thing that came to pass on the Oa, yesterday. And how the wicked murderer of the good and saintly Prior Crispinus met death at his own hands, after confessing his sin."

I wondered at his description of my father as "good and saintly" but guessed that that was how most people would remember him. It was only a few of us that would know the truth of it all; it seemed His Lordship would make sure of that.

I took a sip of my wine, which tasted suddenly bitter, while

His Lordship continued speaking.

"Word has been sent to the Priory, which I myself endowed these twenty years ago and more, that the evil man has been found, and is even now judged by the Heavenly Father himself and meeting Our Lord's own punishment."

A murmur of approval greeted this announcement.

"I think most of you are knowing," he continued, after waiting for the noise to die down again, "that it is the Prior's own son, and nephew to that MacPhee of Colonsay, our own much-loved Gillespic, who was solving the murder and bringing the guilty one to justice. And so for this, I asked the bards to compose the song that you have just heard. Muirteach, come forward."

I am not sure how it was that I got out of my chair and approached His Lordship, who was standing in his place at the center of the high table. But somehow it was that I walked there, feeling all the eyes of the company upon me as I did so.

"Muirteach, we are much pleased by your resolution of this. And for this we award you lands both on Colonsay and in the Rhinns here on Islay, some ten *merks* of good farmland, with houses, and the cattle on them as well."

I thanked him, and he continued, with much eloquence and lordly show.

"In exchange for this we ask only your continued faithful service to us."

I assured him of my loyalty, and thought to return to my place, but His Lordship motioned me to stay and continued speaking.

"In addition to this, as a reward for his faithful service, I now make Muirteach our Keeper of the Records. So that he and his heirs to come will keep and hold the records of the doings of the Council of the Chiefs of the Isles, when we meet at Finlaggan, and the records of other matters as they shall come to pass."

What could I do? Although I wondered somewhat cynically what these "other matters" might entail, I stammered my gratitude, knelt and swore again my loyalty to himself, and then somehow found my way back to my seat.

The Beaton smiled at me, and congratulated me, and I saw Mariota's eyes beaming in the torchlight of the hall.

"Muirteach, that is aye wonderful!" Her nose wrinkled in that way she had that I liked to watch so. "Perhaps the thatch will not be leaking so badly in your new houses as it does in your old cottage."

"And why should you be caring about that?"

She smiled, looking me in the eye. "Och, I am just not liking the thought of you and that great hound of yours dripping wet whenever it is raining."

And with that admission I had to be content.

ABOUT THE AUTHOR

Susan McDuffie has been a fan of all things Scottish, and a devotee of historical fiction, since her childhood. At times she used to wonder if she was mistakenly born in the wrong century, but her discovery that Clorox was not marketed prior to 1922 reconciled her to life in this era. She has visited Scotland several times and done extensive research for *A Mass for the Dead,* which is her first full-length mystery novel. Susan has lived in New Mexico for the past twenty-two years and shares her life with a Native American sculptor and three cats, Dolores, Liam and Finn.